AN ELIGIBLE GENTLEMAN

The Eversley Saga
Book Four

Alice Chetwynd Ley

SAPERE
BOOKS

AN ELIGIBLE GENTLEMAN

Published by Sapere Books.

20 Windermere Drive, Leeds, England, LS17 7UZ,
United Kingdom

saperebooks.com

ISBN: 978-1-80055-419-1

CHAPTER I

The Honourable Frederick Eversley, smartly attired as was his custom in a snug-fitting blue coat fashioned by one of London's foremost tailors, a pair of buff pantaloons, gleaming Hessians and an intricately arranged snowy cravat, stepped from his doorway into Bruton Street. As he did so, he cast a cynical glance at the sky, which was attempting to promise a fine morning by a faint display of watery March sunshine. He decided that he might trust it so far as to walk the short distance to Curzon Street, where his parents' town house was situated.

He had been summoned there by a hastily scrawled, almost illegible note from his mother requesting that he should look in on her as soon as might be convenient. An affectionate son such as the Honourable Frederick unquestionably was might have felt some premonition of a family disaster on observing the wavering handwriting of the note. Mr. Eversley was not perturbed, however, for he recognised it as Lady Eversley's habitually impetuous writing style. He did, in fact, feel a certain mild curiosity concerning the reason for the summons, which was a rare event. The excellent relations existing between the Honourable Frederick and his respected parents owed much to a healthy determination on both sides to respect a mutual desire to pursue independent lives.

Frederick Eversley was a tall, well-built young gentleman of six and twenty, with the aristocratic features and rich tawny hair shared by all the male members of his family. He was a bachelor, as matrimony was a state to which he did not aspire, preferring to flirt discreetly with any attractive young ladies who came his way and who did not display too blatant a desire to catch him, as he phrased it, in parson's mousetrap. There were plenty with this inclination, since his extreme eligibility was certainly not overlooked by hopeful mamas with young daughters in tow. Well-born, personable young gentlemen of fortune were a natural target for these ladies, and he frequently had to exercise his wits in order to avoid their lures.

In disposition he was easy-going and tolerant, but he knew how to deal firmly with those who sought to take advantage of this, mistaking it for weakness. He had been on the town, as the saying went, since attaining his majority, living in a set of comfortable rooms in Bruton Street when in London, and he took part in all the usual diversions of the ton, besides following the more active outdoor pursuits of his own particular cronies. In all, it was a pleasant existence, and he had no desire for change.

The door of his parents' house was opened to him by a lugubrious individual who had been butler to Lord Eversley since the Honourable Frederick was a boy. Having greeted him cheerfully and won in response a reluctant smile, Freddy handed over his hat, cane and gloves and enquired where Lady Eversley might be found.

"My lady is in the morning-room, Mr. Frederick," Timpson replied in measured accents. "Shall I announce you, sir?"

"No need for that," replied Freddy airily. "'Tis a poor thing if I need to be announced to my own mother." He trod confidently across the chequerboard hall, past the white statue of a demure Greek maiden which occupied a small alcove, and paused outside one of the doors, tapping lightly before pushing it open.

"Freddy! How good of you to come!"

The lady seated at a small writing desk in the window rose impetuously on seeing him, scattering the papers on the desk in her haste. She was in her middle fifties but still pleasing to the eye, with delicate features, brown hair flecked with grey, and a particularly warm smile. She stretched out both hands to him. He took them in his, bending to kiss her cheek.

"How are you, Mama? Nothing amiss, I trust? I must say you look in the best of health."

"Oh, no, nothing in the world, my dear," she answered, affectionately returning his kiss. "Both your father and I are in good health, I'm happy to say. But there is a little matter on which I may require your assistance."

"Assistance?" He gave her a quizzical look. "Not getting into deep waters at whist or backgammon, are you? Outrun the constable, what?"

She laughed. "Absurd creature, you know I detest all card games!"

"Backgammon isn't a card game," he said, in the interests of accuracy. "But tell me, Mama, how I may serve you. I'm always happy to oblige, you know."

"Yes, I do know, but perhaps —" She broke off, evidently finding some difficulty in beginning her explanation. "Do sit down, and I'll ring for some refreshment. What will you take?"

Having settled for a glass of madeira, Frederick himself rang the bell. Once he was supplied with this beverage and they were again alone, he raised a questioning eyebrow at his mother. "Well, Mama?"

"The thing is," she began hesitantly, "your Aunt Ianthe has invited all three of us — Papa, myself and you — to stay with her at Chalgrove Park for a few days — longer, if we wish."

"Oh, no!" he exclaimed in disgust.

"I thought you might not quite like it," she said, studying his face, which had set into an obstinate mask. "But it is rather awkward, you see, my dear. You've refused her invitations so often on one pretext or another, and she particularly desires you to go. Your cousin Thomas would like to have you there as his guest. 'Tis a few years now since last you two met."

"No need to be surprised at that. I had enough of young Tom when I had to keep an eye on him at Eton," Frederick answered forcefully. "He's a good enough sort of fellow, of course, but not precisely in my style."

"I fancy you may find him improved. After all, he's three and twenty and has taken on the duties of his estate for several years. I'll admit your aunt has perhaps kept him too close — Phoebe, too — but one can readily understand it, seeing as she was left a widow so young, and with Tom heir to an earldom. It was indeed a prodigious responsibility!"

"You're well aware of my views on that score, Mama. Why, it was as much as Tom could manage to get himself sent to school. Not that I mean to say any boy in his senses would positively yearn to go to Eton," he added, with a reminiscent grin. "Still, it must have been a shade less boring than being kept at home with some dried up old stick of a tutor, which was what she'd originally intended for the poor chap."

"Yes, and if it had not been for her neighbour, Lord Ashcroft — however, I digress. What I wish to say is that it will be especially awkward if you do refuse this invitation, as your father is obliged to do so. He has urgent affairs at our country house which he expects will occupy him for the next few weeks."

"Has he, now?" asked Freddy admiringly. "The crafty old so-and-so!"

"You shouldn't speak so of your father," Lady Eversley said reprovingly, but with a twinkle in her grey eyes. "His business is genuine enough, I assure you. But you must see that if you both refuse —"

He nodded ruefully. "Very well, Mama, I can't let you down. When do you intend to go?"

She gave a sigh of relief and pressed his hand. "I knew I could rely on you, Freddy. I shall plan the visit to suit your convenience, naturally, since I realise you will already have engagements. Your aunt did suggest next week, but —" She paused expectantly.

Freddy made a rapid mental review of his social commitments, decided that there was nothing pressing, then nodded. "Suits me. But I don't intend to remain there beyond the week, mind," he warned her. "A little of my Aunt Chalgrove goes a long way with me."

Lady Eversley allowed this impolite remark to pass, too pleased at having gained her way. "Oh, yes, I think we may be able to make this a short visit, as the real object of it is for me to bring Phoebe back with me to town."

"My cousin Phoebe?" he asked, surprised. "But she's still a chit in the schoolroom, isn't she?"

She laughed. "Oh, no, you're forgetting how long it is since you last saw her. She's eighteen now and ready to go into society. In fact, she has been out for some months, but theirs is a restricted neighbourhood, and your aunt became persuaded that Phoebe ought to be introduced into the wider circle of acquaintance available to her with us in London."

"Very understandable. No doubt she's thinking of a suitable match for the girl."

"That does come into it, certainly," Lady Eversley replied, avoiding his eye so that he wondered fleetingly just what she was keeping up her sleeve.

"I must say, it seems a trifle hard on you to be obliged to go racketing about the town with a young girl, years after you've already seen off two daughters of your own," Freddy said indignantly. "What was to prevent Aunt Chalgrove from taking a house here herself for the season? I dare say my cousin Tom would have welcomed a change from Chalgrove Park, too."

"Surely you must realise by now that my sister has the greatest dislike of leaving her own home? She and the late earl never did so, and as she was married straight from the schoolroom, she's never known any other way of life."

"All the same, it's twelve years since the late earl passed on," said Freddy flippantly. "Most females in her case would have launched out a trifle since then."

"So I have tried to persuade her, but to no avail. She keeps on in the same old way. And as for letting Thomas loose on the town, even Lord Ashcroft hasn't been able to influence her on that subject, though I understand he's tried."

"Poor devil," said Freddy commiseratingly. "Must be frightful to be tied to a parent's apron strings. Not that I don't consider he should show more spirit."

"He is very fond of his mama, and will do nothing to vex her. Besides," added Lady Eversley, weakening sufficiently to admit a slight criticism of her sister, "you know how your Aunt Ianthe has the trick of shaming people into giving way to her."

"I most certainly do," returned Freddy fervently, "which is exactly why I do my best to avoid visiting Chalgrove Park. But just this once, Mama, to oblige you... I'm not sure," he finished, with an impudent grin, "that your sister's trait doesn't run in the family, you know."

"Wretch! I declare this is the first time that I have ever tried to persuade you to anything you disliked."

"Well, not quite the first," he said judicially, "though I'll grant such occasions are fortunately rare enough." He drew out his fob watch and consulted it. "I regret I must leave you now, Mama, so perhaps we'd best get down to business. When do you wish to set out for Sussex?"

This and other minor points being settled amicably, Mr. Eversley took leave of his gratified parent, and proceeded on his way to Brooks' Club in St. James' Street. Here he found several sporting gentlemen of his acquaintance gathered in one of the saloons, bending over the book in which it was customary to record members' often outrageous wagers.

"What's to do?" he demanded of one of the group.

"Only that Chartley's just accepted a wager to attend Almack's in trousers and a crimson waistcoat," replied the other, with a chuckle. "Must have been foxed when he made it. He knows he won't get past the door."

"Good heavens, no, he won't," agreed Freddy, amused.

Correct evening attire for that exclusive haunt of fashion, Almack's Assembly Rooms, amounted almost to a uniform, comprising knee breeches, a dark coloured tailcoat and a waistcoat of pristine white. The rules laid down by the committee of ladies who reigned over this establishment were so stringent that even the Prince of Wales himself would have been refused admission had he sought to attend an assembly improperly dressed.

"I dare say it will shake them up a trifle, though," continued his informant, a man named Doughton. "Some of us intend going along to watch."

Freddy shrugged. "He'll lose his money, of course, but otherwise 'tis no real hardship to be denied admission to

Almack's — slowest place I was ever in! Dare say you feel the same. Most of us do."

Doughton agreed heartily, and Freddy moved away into one of the other rooms. Here he was greeted by Viscount Pamyngton, a tall, fair-haired gentleman a few years his senior who was a close friend of Freddy's eldest brother.

"Haven't seen you lately, Freddy," said Pamyngton, "and my wife was asking after you only the other day. Why don't you come and dine with us one day next week?"

"I'd have been only too happy," returned Freddy, his face clouding momentarily, "but the trouble is I'm obliged to accompany my mother into Sussex to visit some dashed relatives."

"Sussex? Would that be the Chalgroves, by any chance?" asked Pamyngton.

"Yes, it is. Oh, I forgot — of course you'll be acquainted with them, as your people live in the same neighbourhood. Have you met my cousin Thomas, the present earl? He's a good bit younger than you, of course."

Pamyngton shook his head. "Not since he was a grubby schoolboy, and even then only infrequently. My parents aren't near neighbours of theirs, and the late earl was not a man greatly given to socialising. I believe the dowager countess behaves in much the same way?"

Freddy nodded gloomily. "Heaven knows what I've let myself in for — improving readings round the fireside of an evening, I shouldn't wonder!"

Pamyngton laughed. "Well, I dare say it won't be as bad as you fear. Tell you what, if you feel in need of a change of company, why don't you call on the Denhams — my wife's family, you know? They live close by, and Sir George will make you welcome. Remember Eleanor, my wife's younger sister?

She's still at home, and you two got on famously together when we were all in Brighton two years ago. She's a lively girl, Nell."

The Honourable Frederick wrinkled his brow in thought for a moment. A great deal of water had passed under the bridge in two years, and girls came and went without leaving much impression upon his carefree bachelor existence. He did recollect something, however, now he put his mind to it — an incident to do with a fairground. He chuckled. "By Jove, yes, I do recall her!" he exclaimed triumphantly. "A little schoolroom chit, up to no end of larks. But doubtless she's changed by now, and settled into the usual model of maidenly propriety."

"I wouldn't count on that," replied Pamyngton drily.

CHAPTER II

The room in most frequent use by the family at Chalgrove Park was the Green Salon, not unnaturally so called because of its decor of pastel green walls and a white ceiling tastefully picked out in green and pink after the style of Adam. On the day when Lady Eversley and her son Frederick were expected to arrive, the Dowager Countess of Chalgrove was seated alone in this room at her embroidery frame.

The dowager countess did not at all resemble the usual picture of a dowager. The head bent over her work was crowned by a dainty cap of lace from beneath which appeared locks of the palest gold, owing nothing to artificial aids. Her complexion of pink and white was as smooth as a girl's, her eyes were the blue of cornflowers, and the slender neck rising from the frilled ruff of her elegant grey morning gown showed not the faintest hint of a wrinkle. Her figure, though not perhaps as slim as in girlhood, was nevertheless trim and neat, and when she permitted it to be seen, she possessed a very shapely ankle. She was in fact one of the most attractive matrons to be met with in the county, as her neighbour Baron Ashcroft was never tired of telling anyone who could be brought to listen to him. She was the youngest female of her own family, so was considerably junior to her sister Lady Eversley, having, as her brother-in-law somewhat inelegantly phrased it, only two and forty years in her dish.

Although to all outward appearances she was calm and tranquil, plying her needle in leisurely fashion, inwardly her thoughts were racing. There had been a certain matter on her mind for weeks now, and she felt that the time had come to

14

give voice to it. It was an affair of some delicacy, but she never doubted her ability to handle it successfully.

The ring of riding boots on the marble floor of the hall came to her ears, and the next moment her son Thomas, Fourth Earl of Chalgrove, entered the room. He greeted her punctiliously, as though they had not already met once that day at breakfast, then flung himself down exuberantly into a wing chair.

"I told William to bring me some ale," he said, throwing out his booted legs before him. "I dare say you don't care for anything just now, do you, Mama? It's a splendid morning — let's hope it holds up for the hunt."

She refused the offer, as he had known she would, and laid aside her needle to give him her full attention, moving into a chair close to him. "Did you see Mellor about the thatching?" she asked in her low, sweet voice. "He was anxious to have your decision, I know."

"Oh, yes," he replied casually — a shade too casually for her liking, as was evident by the tiniest suggestion of a frown on that unruffled brow — "but there was really no need for him to wait on my word. He's a first-rate land agent, as I don't need to tell you, Mama, and quite capable of determining these routine matters for himself, without troubling me over them."

"I do not like to think, my dear Tom, that you find any duties of your estate too trivial for your personal attention," she said, in tones of gentle reproof.

"No, no, of course not! I only meant that he knows so much more about such things than I — well, it stands to reason, doesn't it, when he's been our land agent since ever I can remember? And no one can call into question his devotion to our interests."

"As you say, he is a truly devoted servant," she replied in an equable tone. "But even such a one needs to have the full co-operation of the landowner. Did the business take so long?" she continued in a livelier voice. "I had thought to see you back earlier."

His fair complexion betrayed a slight flush. "Oh, no, we soon settled that, and then I went for a ride with Nell — Miss Denham. We chanced to meet in the lane leading to Eastridge House." He tried to throw this off casually, but she was not deceived. She knew quite well that he must have been on his way to the Denhams' house, and he was aware that she knew it.

"I gather Eleanor Denham was about to ride out with her groom?" She had already guessed the answer to this, but had her own reasons for asking it.

Tom looked uneasy. "No, not precisely, but she's a capital horsewoman, as you know, Mama, and sees no need of a groom to accompany her in this neighbourhood."

"I should have supposed that Lady Denham would have insisted upon it, for propriety's sake," Lady Chalgrove said quietly, ignoring the defensive look on her son's face. "I trust you enjoyed your ride. Did you go far?"

"Only to Oakland Common. Yes, it was capital, thank you, Mama — a splendid morning for riding!"

She nodded, smiling. "I am so glad you enjoyed it. While we are on this subject, Tom, there is just one thing I would like to mention."

He looked up sharply, for he knew his parent too well to be deceived by the gentleness of her tone. She meant to give him a raking-down, he thought ruefully, and was at no loss to guess the cause.

"Of course, it is not for me to interfere with any pleasure of yours," she continued, with a deprecating smile. "You are your own master and, moreover, the head of our little household. But I like to think that the affection existing between us will not be unduly strained if I venture to give you just the tiniest hint."

"No, of course not — that's to say, you know I'm always grateful for your advice," he replied awkwardly, and not entirely truthfully.

"I knew it must be so, and it gives me courage to say what I fear may not quite please you," she went on, in honeyed accents. "It does seem to me, my dear, that lately you have been seeing overmuch of Miss Denham."

He flushed to the roots of his flaxen hair, suddenly looking very young and vulnerable, in spite of his twenty-three years. He sat up stiffly in his chair. "But she's Phoebe's friend, so it's only natural that we should often be in company together! Besides, I like her — prodigiously," he added defiantly, "and I thought you liked her, too. Has something occurred to make you change your mind, Mama?"

"Not as to her character, no. I believe her to be a very good sort of a girl," said Lady Chalgrove, in a tone of faint praise more condemnatory than an outright tirade against the absent young lady. "But it will not do to raise the kind of expectations which must come readily to the mind of any young lady whom you choose to honour with your attentions. You are what is vulgarly termed a very good catch, my son."

"Oh, yes, I suppose so," he answered, with an angry shrug. "But, Mama, I must marry someday, so why not —"

She interrupted him swiftly. "Of course, but that time is not yet. You are far too young to be thinking of marriage. And when you do, I trust it will be to some lady of consequence who will make you a fitting countess, not a country miss who thinks nothing of roaming the lanes with mud on her petticoat, or else following the hunt in reckless fashion."

Tom was silent for a moment, fighting down his anger. One must never lose one's temper with Mama, as any kind of scene brought on one of her headaches. All the same, it required a strong effort to answer her calmly. "I don't know how you think I shall meet such a young lady," he said at last, somewhat petulantly. "Certainly there seems to be no one hereabouts whom you consider suitable."

This was true enough, for the earl was an impressionable young man and had taken a fancy to several other females in the neighbourhood before fixing his eyes upon Miss Denham. His mother's disapproval had quickly nipped these promising relationships in the bud, but this time his feelings were more serious.

"If only you'd allow me to go up to London for a spell, as Ashcroft suggests," he continued, in the same aggrieved tone, "there might be some opportunity of that kind. But you won't have it at any price, so what's the use?"

"My dear Tom, I am only thinking — as, indeed, I always am — of your best interests," she replied, in anguished tones. "London is full of snares for an inexperienced young nobleman from the country. I could never know an easy moment, were you to take up residence there. Besides, there is the estate. You do not wish to become one of these negligent absentee landlords, I suppose?"

"No, of course not, but I don't see where the harm would be in my passing a month or two in London every so often. Mellor is more than competent to oversee the estate without me, you know that well. We might have a town house, as most people of consequence do."

"Impossible!" declared Lady Chalgrove, in a much more decisive tone than she normally used. "Your dear papa never found it at all necessary to do so. He was only too content to remain here at home, and I did believe —" she was wistful now — "that you would be of the same mind."

"That's all very well, but one doesn't always wish to go on in the same way," he protested. "Everyone likes a change now and then."

"I do not," she said sadly. "All I want is to remain here in the house I came to as a bride all those years ago, with my family about me."

"Then why are you sending Phoebe to London with my Aunt Eversley?" he demanded, aggrieved. "Seems to me a poor thing if my sister's to go jaunting off, while I am obliged to remain at home."

"I have a particular reason for permitting Phoebe to go," she replied repressively.

"Aye, and I can guess what it is, I suppose. You hope she'll make a good match, and no man hereabouts will do. Not," he added with a puzzled frown, "that I should have thought you'd have objected to a local suitor, since then she'd have resided near at hand."

"You would have been right, had there been any gentleman of this neighbourhood to whom I would gladly give my child," said Lady Chalgrove sententiously. "But what I have in mind, should it happily come to pass, would still keep your sister among us. But I mean to say no more on that subject," she added hurriedly, seeing a question taking form on his lips, "so pray don't tease me, Tom. Already I can feel one of my headaches coming on, and our visitors are due in a few hours. I think I shall go and lie down for a while."

"I am sorry, Mama, if I've vexed you," he said in quick contrition. "I did not mean to do so — forgive me. Shall I ring for Palmer?"

Lady Chalgrove agreed to this suggestion in the failing accents of one about to go off any minute into a swoon. Leaping to his feet with an anxious look, he summoned the maid, and presently his mother left the room leaning gracefully on Palmer's arm, while the latter darted a reproachful glance at the head of the house.

The countess appeared to have made a recovery little short of miraculous, however, less than half an hour later when Lord Ashcroft came to call.

This gentleman was a privileged visitor at Chalgrove Park; indeed, almost one of the family. His property adjoined that of the Chalgroves', though it was not as extensive. In consequence, he and the late earl had grown up together. Since his friend's death twelve years previously, he had kept a paternal eye on the bereaved family, and was the only person to whose advice Lady Chalgrove ever paid the slightest heed. He had stood as godfather to Thomas and Phoebe, and was on excellent terms with both.

He came into the room with a firm step, greeting her cheerfully. He was a distinguished-looking, well-built man in his late forties, with dark hair touched at the temples with grey, a frank, open countenance and a pair of lively but shrewd grey eyes.

"Gathering your strength for the arrival of your visitors, Ianthe?" he quizzed, seeing her sitting with idle hands, staring pensively into the middle distance.

She smiled up at him in a way that still had the power to make his heart turn over. It was not unlikely that she was aware of this. "Not quite that, for 'tis only my own sister, after all. But I have been a trifle upset by Tom," she added plaintively.

"What's the young devil been up to?" he asked, taking a chair in his usual easy way. "Some mischief, eh? Time he did break out a little, mind you — only natural, at his age."

"Oh, no, don't say so!" she begged, obviously horrified by this remark. "No, 'tis not mischief, precisely. Only he's been asking me again to allow him to go to London."

He gave her a direct look. "Well, you're already acquainted with my views on that topic, so I won't vex you by repeating them."

She gave him a fluttering, helpless glance from her deep blue eyes. It might have taken in a man less well acquainted with her, but Henry Ashcroft knew that there was nothing in the least helpless about the dowager countess, who could be as inflexible as she was beautiful. His knowledge of her true character did not at all diminish his feelings for her. He was above all a realist, prepared to accept the foibles of others, and particularly those of Ianthe Chalgrove.

"But you must surely understand that I should be failing in my duty towards my son, were I to submit him to the pitfalls lying in wait for an inexperienced young nobleman in such a place as London."

"As to your duty to Tom," he replied, more gently than before, "you may reasonably feel that it was discharged on the day he attained his majority. He now needs to think and act for himself, and can only remedy his inexperience by emerging into the wider world outside his own house."

"You mean that you consider he no longer needs me?" she asked, with a trembling lip.

He leaned over to pat her hand briefly but affectionately. "He needs family affection, of course — we all do. But there comes a time when youngsters must go their own way and parents must accept it with a good grace. You're still a comparatively young woman, my dear Ianthe, and can make a satisfactory life for yourself independently of your family, if you choose." He stopped himself abruptly at this point.

She made no reply, staring somewhat bleakly before her.

"Still, I don't intend to lecture," he continued, in a lighter tone, "else you'll be wishing me elsewhere. You'll like having your sister with you for a few days. It will cheer you up to have some female company besides young Phoebe. I dare say Tom will be pleased to have his cousin here, too — sensible young fellow, Freddy Eversley. I like him."

"Oh, so do I, vastly," Lady Chalgrove replied, recovering her spirits at once. "I don't mind admitting to you, Harry, that the real reason I wished Phoebe to go and stay with my sister in London — but there, you're so astute, I'm sure you can hazard a guess."

"Hm, perhaps I may," he said dubiously. "But, as a matter of fact, I rather think that young Lydhurst —"

"Geoffrey Lydhurst? Impossible!" declared Lady Chalgrove emphatically. "He will not do at all for Phoebe."

"Can't think why not," protested Ashcroft. "He's a fine young chap — capital sportsman. There's no shortage of money, and his expectations are good — he'll have Lydhurst Manor one day. Besides, his sister and little Phoebe are bosom friends, aren't they? The whole family's fond of my goddaughter. I should have supposed you'd have preferred her to marry into a local family, too."

"Phoebe is a beauty — I'm sure you'll not deny *that* — and can do better for herself than wed a country squire's son. Besides, there's no saying where Geoffrey Lydhurst would choose to reside when he marries. It will be many years before he comes into the property, for Sir Bertram is no older than you are yourself, and a hale and hearty man."

"Well, we shall see," he extemporised, reluctant to carry the argument further at this stage. He had never been one to flog a dead horse.

CHAPTER III

The Honourable Frederick Eversley's first evening at Chalgrove Park did nothing to dispel his gloomy forebodings that the visit would prove a dead bore. At first, he was agreeably surprised that his cousin, Lady Phoebe, whom he recalled as an undersized, skinny schoolgirl, was now transformed into a slender, ethereal beauty with ringlets of the palest gold and a heart-shaped face from which gazed a pair of wide, innocent blue eyes. His interest in this pleasing metamorphosis soon evaporated, however, when he found her almost as shy and retiring as of yore, evidently not the girl with whom a fellow might reasonably expect to share even the very mildest of flirtations.

Lady Eversley several times repeated, to the embarrassment of Phoebe and the boredom of most of her hearers, that her niece was the image of her mama at the same age. Accustomed as he was to his mother's habit of tracing the most unlikely family resemblances in this way, Freddy was obliged to allow that for once there really was something in it.

There was less physical change in his cousin Thomas, who had always been a good-looking youth. Maturity had added breadth of shoulder to his tall, slim figure; and the critical eyes cast by his cousin could find no fault in the cut of his coat, nor in the fashionable styling of his blond hair. It remained to be discovered whether he would prove a more lively companion than in former years.

During an excellent dinner, the talk was entirely of family matters, never a favourite topic with Freddy. By the time the ladies retired to leave the gentlemen with what he acknowledged to his host was a more than tolerable wine, the reluctant guest was hard put to it to stifle his yawns. Tom's conversation was less tedious away from the rest of the family, however, and Freddy brightened considerably at the mention of a day's hunting later in the week. A return to the drawing-room brought on his previous sufferings, which were only alleviated, after the appearance of the tea tray, by a happy suggestion from Thomas that they should both repair to the billiard-room. It was an extremely dull evening, reflected Freddy ruefully when he eventually retired to bed, and doubtless a pattern of what was in store for the duration of the visit.

Although when in London it was not Freddy's habit to be seen out in the early hours of the morning, in the country, matters were different. Town noises never disturbed him; but in the country cockerels crowed, birds twittered, sheep bleated, cattle lowed, all in a concerted animal chorus which impinged on the ear to force the sluggard's attention to the dawning of another day. After doing his best to ignore the summons, he finally succumbed with an oath to nature's importunity at what his town friends would have unhesitatingly considered an unreasonable hour. He dressed and made his way to the breakfast-room.

He found Thomas there alone, just finishing his meal. His cousin looked startled on seeing him.

"Didn't think you'd be down for another hour or two, Freddy," he said apologetically. "I've some business with my land agent that can't wait, and I'd hoped to get it concluded in time to join you after you'd breakfasted. Do you care to accompany me? I can easily wait while you have your meal."

Freddy waved a dismissive hand. "No, no, old chap, you go. I might try out the paces of that mount you offered me when we were chatting last night — that's if you've no objection?"

"Not the least in the world," answered Tom, rising from the table. "'Tis a smart bay, and I think you'll like it. I'm off to the stables now, so I'll tell my head groom to expect you shortly. When I get back, you might care to look over the rest of my horseflesh? I've one or two prime bits of stock, and I'd value your opinion."

This being settled, he departed, leaving his cousin to a solitary breakfast, for none of the ladies had as yet put in an appearance. Far from feeling this as a hardship, Freddy welcomed a respite from the doubtful delights of family conversation; and later, when he was riding down the winding drive towards open country, he enjoyed much the same sensations as might a boy who had been released for a time from school.

Less than three miles away, at Eastridge House, Sir George and Lady Denham were also sitting over breakfast with their three daughters and the governess. The two younger girls, Jane and Olivia, aged fifteen and thirteen respectively, were carefully minding their manners so far as to refrain from quizzing their mama about the letter she was reading, even though they knew it was from their sister, Lady Pamyngton, in London, and they were longing to hear her news. Their nineteen-year-old sister, Eleanor, freed long ago from the tutelage of a governess, had no such inhibitions, however.

"Don't be so monstrously secretive, Mama, pray!" she exclaimed with a laugh that lit up her expressive hazel eyes. "Can't you see we're all dying to hear what Katie says? Read it aloud, do."

Lady Denham looked up with a severe glance. "Pray curb your curiosity, Eleanor. You set a poor example to your younger sisters. Besides, I must first read it myself to make quite certain that it contains nothing improper for your ears."

"*Improper*! A letter from Katie!" exclaimed Eleanor incredulously. "Oh, fudge, Mama!"

Sir George gave a choke of laughter which he hastily turned into a cough as he saw his wife's reproachful eye upon him. "Mustn't speak to your mother like that," he said half-heartedly to his favourite daughter. "Not at all the thing, you know, Nell."

"No, well, I'm sorry, Mama. But do please hurry up and give us Katie's news — *please*."

Thus appealed to, Lady Denham allowed herself to be mollified. After all, she was reasonably in charity with Eleanor at present, as the girl had lately been receiving the flattering attentions of none other than the highly eligible Earl of Chalgrove. The mother of six daughters, Lady Denham's chief preoccupation had always been the procuring of suitable husbands for those of her brood who were of an age to require such provision. She had succeeded in establishing her three eldest — Catherine's marriage to Viscount Pamyngton had so far represented her greatest triumph — and now only Eleanor was in imminent need of her efforts in that direction. She smiled frostily.

"You will be glad to hear that your sister and Pamyngton are in good health, also that baby Gerard is thriving," she began, glancing at the letter. "She has just purchased a most delightful pink satin ball gown, very low cut —" here she glanced apprehensively at her two youngest — "and caught up at the hem with tiny rosebuds. Oh, and there's more about fashions, but you may read that for yourselves later. We must not inflict such stuff upon Papa. She repeats some of the gossip current in ton circles — well, really, I wouldn't have supposed that even Mr. Brummell would venture to say *that* to His Royal Highness!" she declared, breaking off her recital, evidently much shocked.

"Say what, Mama?" queried Eleanor, agog with curiosity. "Pray do go on!"

Lady Denham folded the letter and laid it aside. "I shall permit you to read it for yourself after breakfast, Eleanor, for there is a paragraph at the end which particularly concerns you. But you two —" she nodded towards Jane and Olivia — "must be content with what you've already heard."

Their faces fell, but recollecting after a moment that they could easily persuade their sister to reveal the full content of the letter when Mama was not there, they soon recovered and presently rose from the table to follow their governess from the room. Sir George also departed, leaving Eleanor and his wife together. Eleanor at once snatched up the letter with what her mother condemned as unseemly haste, and was soon deep in a perusal punctuated by chuckles and an occasional hearty laugh. Her manner changed, however, on arriving at the final paragraph.

"Oh, Mama, Katie invites me to stay with her for a month or so — the whole season, if I wish! Isn't that capital? I should like it better than anything, now the hunting's almost over."

"I think you would be very foolish to go away at present," replied Lady Denham. "I don't wish it."

"Oh, but why?" her daughter protested.

"Only consider, my dear. Chalgrove has been paying you most particular attentions of late, and to remove yourself from his vicinity at this juncture could ruin it all. There's no overlooking the fact that he's an impressionable young man, and with most of the girls in the county setting their caps at him, there's no saying that he might not fall victim to someone else."

"Pooh!" exclaimed Eleanor scornfully. "He can't have formed a very strong attachment if a short absence would cause him to forget me. Besides, Mama, I'm not at all sure that I wish to wed Tom — or, indeed, anyone, at present."

"Then you are foolish beyond belief. You are turned nineteen and must soon be thinking of marriage, come what may, for even you with your odd notions cannot wish to become an old maid. And you will never again have the opportunity of such an advantageous match, allow me to tell you. Just think of it, my dear, an *earl*. Katie's having wed a viscount will be nothing compared with it — and when you were younger, you once said how much you should like to be a countess."

"Oh, Mama! You know what nonsense one talks at seventeen," replied Eleanor, with a scornful laugh for her less mature self. "Besides, I was only joking, even then. I am not at all sure, now," she went on, in a more serious voice, "that one should ever marry without a strong — partiality — for the person concerned." She had been about to use the word "love" but fought shy of it at the last moment. Lady Denham had never encouraged her girls in what she would condemn as foolishly romantic notions.

"You *do* have a partiality for Chalgrove," persisted her mother. "You're often enough in his company, and you seem to get on extremely well together."

"I'm often in his company, naturally, since his sister is one of my close friends."

"You are not trying to pretend that you don't like the young man himself, surely?" countered Lady Denham impatiently.

"No such thing — of course I like Tom. After all, I've been acquainted with him for most of my life."

"Precisely. Which is just the reason why a match between you would be eminently suitable. It is far better to know something of your husband before marriage, believe me."

"Perhaps so, Mama, but it is not very exciting to marry someone whom one knows so well."

Lady Denham delivered herself of a contemptuous exclamation which in a lesser woman might have been called a snort. "Exciting, indeed! I should suppose you would find enough excitement in being elevated to the rank of countess. It would certainly satisfy the majority of females. And I tell you now, Eleanor, that if you let such an opportunity slip through your fingers, I'll have done with you!"

Eleanor's fair skin flushed with anger. "That's a pity, Mama, but I'll not be coerced in such a matter. I must decide for myself!"

She swept from the room and ran upstairs to change hurriedly into her riding dress. By far the best way to shake off the irritation of a tiff with Mama, as she knew from recent experience, was to go for a gallop over the fields. As she made her way to the stables, she reflected wryly that these tiffs had been more frequent lately. It was partly her own fault, she acknowledged. Mama's notions of propriety were stricter than her own, and she did tend to act impulsively. But perhaps it was simply that some friction was inevitable between a mother and a daughter of her age. Doubtless it was time, as Mama had often said of late, for her to be thinking of marriage. In the end, Eleanor admitted, she might well decide to marry Tom, should his attentions prove serious. But he was still young — younger in many ways than most men of his age — and decidedly impressionable where females were concerned, as his past erratic fancies had shown. However that might be, she had not the slightest intention of allowing her hand to be forced.

She was soon mounted on a sleek chestnut mare, a recent acquisition which she had taken out only a few times before, and which had what her groom described as a restless temperament. This did not at all worry Eleanor, who was an excellent rider, and prided herself on her ability to manage any horse. Once in the meadows, she gave the mare its head, revelling in the swift rush through the air and the exhilarating sense of freedom it brought. She began to feel better already, her irritation falling away from her.

Eventually she reached the point where the stretch of meadowland ended in a hedge bordering the lane which led back in one direction to Eastridge House. There was a gate situated a short distance from her, but she did not propose to trouble herself to make for this. Instead, she steered the mare towards the hedge. The animal prepared to take the obstacle easily in its stride, but in mid-air Eleanor suddenly let out a cry of alarm and tugged instinctively on the rein in what was a useless attempt to check the jump.

Too late, she had seen that another rider was almost directly beneath her. A collision seemed inevitable. Fortunately, the rider acted promptly, forcing his horse over to the opposite side of the lane just in time to avert the danger.

Confused by its rider's attempted check, Eleanor's mount made an awkward landing half in the muddy ditch. At once it showed its disapproval of her tactics by rearing violently. She clutched frantically at its neck in a vain effort to retain her seat, then slipped ignominiously from the saddle into the muddy ditch.

The horseman swiftly dismounted and ran towards her. "Are you hurt?" he demanded, as he assisted her to her feet.

"No — never mind me!" she gasped, shaking off his solicitous hold and darting forward to try and seize her plunging, terrified horse. "The mare!"

"Stand aside, ma'am — leave her to me," he ordered curtly, grasping the mare's bridle at some risk from thrashing hoofs.

Eleanor did as he bade her. She was somewhat shaken by her fall, though otherwise unhurt, but in spite of her confused state she was still able to feel some resentment at his manner, which she considered too high-handed by half. Nevertheless, she watched with grudging admiration his expert handling of the animal, while she stood nearby, gradually recovering her breath.

Although he obviously knew what he was doing, it took some time to quieten the nervous creature. Once he had succeeded in this, he walked it up and down, running a keen eye over it as he did so.

"You're more fortunate than you deserve," he said grimly, turning to Eleanor. "Your mare's not hurt, small thanks to you. What of yourself, ma'am? You're quite sure you've sustained no injury?"

She drew herself up to what was meant to be a dignified stance, but she could scarcely have realised what an undignified appearance she actually presented. Her pretty blue riding habit was plastered with mud and she had lost her hat in the ditch. Moreover, her hair had come loose from its pins and was trailing wetly against her mud-streaked face. "I take exception to your tone, sir!" she snapped.

He gave her a half-amused look. "What do you expect, when you deuced nearly landed on top of me? Do you make a practice, ma'am, of jumping hedges without first ascertaining if there's any unfortunate on the other side? If so, I wonder this countryside isn't positively littered with corpses."

She looked a trifle nonplussed. "No, of course not. The thing is, I didn't hear you approaching —"

"Hard of hearing, what?" he asked, with spurious sympathy. "A sad affliction, and you not yet stricken in years."

She gasped in indignation, glaring at him with what he noticed were remarkably eloquent hazel eyes. She tried to keep her tone calm, however. "The thing is, I was a trifle abstracted at the time. I suppose," she said reluctantly, "I owe you an apology."

"Say no more on the subject, ma'am," he said generously. "But are you sure you're unhurt?"

"Perfectly. I may have a bruise or two later, but that's of no account." She bent over the ditch to retrieve her high-crowned riding hat, holding it up with an expression of distaste. This, too, was daubed with mud, and the feathers which had formerly adorned it now drooped forlornly. She heard the horseman let out a half-choked laugh, and swung, red-faced, towards him. "I am delighted to be privileged to cause you so much amusement!" she snapped, cramming the hat on her head.

He grimaced ruefully. "My turn to apologise, ma'am. Afraid I've an unfortunate sense of humour."

As Eleanor herself was frequently accused of possessing this same fault, she might well have joined him at this point in laughing over her recent mishap, but he went on immediately to make another highly provocative remark.

"This mare of yours," he said, running his free hand over the now docile animal's neck, "prime bit of stock, but I'd say too high-spirited for a lady's mount."

"You are quite mistaken. I would have you know, sir, that I am well up to form where horsemanship is concerned. Naturally, 'tis not for me to boast, but I may tell you that I regularly ride to hounds, and I haven't taken a tumble like this in years."

"Well, if you feel sufficiently recovered now, ma'am," he replied placatingly, "I'll put you up in the saddle and then do myself the honour of escorting you home, wherever that may be."

"I live at Eastridge House, only a mile or so along this lane. As to escorting me home, I thank you, but there's not the least need of that," she said stiffly.

"Eastridge House?" he repeated, surprised. "Ah, that explains it — I've been thinking all along that I recognised you, but scarcely liked to ask if we hadn't met before. You might have supposed," he went on, laughing at her in an attempt to win an amused response, "that I was making use of a hackneyed old gambit for scraping acquaintance with a lady."

From her aloof expression, he saw that his little jest was not to succeed. Recognition had shown in her eyes, however.

"You're Miss Eleanor Denham," he went on quickly, hoping to thaw the icy temperature. "And I'm Frederick Eversley. You may recollect we first met when I was staying in this neighbourhood a few years ago with my friend Pamyngton, who is now married to one of your sisters. We also met again a few weeks later, during your visit to Brighton. Dare I hope that you still remember me? I don't think I've changed much since then."

She had to admit that this was true. Although the eye with which she was regarding him at that moment was decidedly jaundiced, she went so far as to allow that the rich auburn hair, a firm chin, humorous mouth and quizzing brown eyes, together with an elegant yet athletic figure, all amounted to a most personable gentleman. She did remember him, now that she had leisure to consider the matter, and she also recollected that they had dealt extremely well together during those brief past encounters. Nevertheless, at present she was not disposed to show him any favour. She told herself that he had been unpardonably rude to her, and she was reluctant to admit that he might have had sufficient provocation. She nodded coldly. "Yes, I do recollect you, Mr. Eversley. I shall be obliged if you will assist me to mount, but after that I require no further service of you."

"No, deuce take it, I can't do such a thing as to let you return home unescorted after you've just taken a tumble," he protested.

She made no answer, but set her lips in a firm line as she moved towards the mare. He gave her the reins, then, before she could guess his intention or make any attempt to prevent it, he placed his hands about her waist, swinging her lightly to the saddle.

Her cheeks were flushed as she settled herself there, adjusting her skirts before giving the mare the order to start. She at once moved away, but a backward glance showed that he had mounted and was coming up to her side. Her eyes flashed. "I thought I'd made it plain that I don't desire your escort!" she flung at him.

"Very plain, Miss Denham," he answered cheerfully. "But I feel it my duty to accompany you."

"Very well. I can see no way of escaping your company, but pray don't expect me to converse with you!" she exclaimed hotly.

"A sad deprivation, seeing as you're so much in charity with me, ma'am. But I shall use my best endeavours to survive it."

The look she gave him ought, by rights, to have caused him to fall lifeless from his horse, but he answered it with an unconcerned grin.

So they rode, side by side, in silence until they reached the gates of Eastridge House, where Eleanor dismissed him with a frigid inclination of her head.

Eleanor had hoped to creep into the house unobserved by her mother, but unluckily Lady Denham crossed the hall at the precise moment that her daughter was about to ascend the staircase.

"Merciful heavens!" she exclaimed in horrified accents, falling back a pace and staring at the dishevelled and muddy apparition before her. "What in the world have you been doing, Eleanor? Your dress — your hair — your *hair* —"

"I took a tumble, that's all," replied Eleanor in a casual tone. "No need to make a tragedy out of it, Mama — I didn't hurt myself, so there's no harm done beyond muddying my clothes." She was proceeding to run upstairs, but halted reluctantly as her mother's aggrieved voice continued its plaint.

"Took a tumble! That is not at all like you, for I must say that if you do possess one accomplishment, it is that you're an excellent horsewoman. How did it come about? Surely you mean to explain what happened?"

"Oh, not now, Mama. Can't you see that I need to change at once? I'll tell you presently."

"Yes, of course," answered Lady Denham, seeing the sense of this. "But pray don't be too long about it, Eleanor, for your friend Phoebe is here, waiting to see you. She's been sitting with me this half hour or more — such an inconvenient time to call," she added in an undertone, with a furtive glance towards a door opening off the hall. "I had no notion when I might expect you to return, for you never tell me where you are going. Oh, very well, off with you, and come down as soon as possible. We're in the morning-room."

With the assistance of her scandalised maid, it did not take Eleanor very long to emerge clean and fresh from her bedchamber. It had been necessary to wash her hair, however, so when she finally presented herself in the morning-room, a small towel was draped in the manner of a turban about her head.

Phoebe took one look at this headgear and broke into a laugh, quickly stifled as she glanced apologetically at her friend in fear of giving offence.

"Yes, I do look a sight, don't I?" remarked Eleanor cheerfully. "But you should have seen me when I came in, my dear. Mama nearly had a fit."

"Small wonder," said Lady Denham acidly. "I suppose this was just another of your wild starts, but I should like to know precisely what occurred to make you fall from your horse."

"Oh, I was jumping the hedge, but there was another rider on the other side," explained Eleanor airily. "I tried to pull back at the last minute to avoid a collision, but the mare didn't like it and decanted me into the ditch. No harm done."

Phoebe exclaimed in commiseration. A timid horsewoman herself, never allowed out unless with a groom or other suitable escort, the mere thought of a tumble made her quail.

"What of the other rider?" demanded Eleanor's mother. "I gather from your tone that luckily it was not one of our acquaintances?"

"Oh, no," answered Eleanor quickly, unwilling to explain just who it had been. "Never fear, he came off completely unscathed. But Phoebe does not want to listen to this, Mama, when I dare say she called to tell me something on her own account. If we must discuss this, could we not do so later?"

Lady Denham rose. "Very well. I dare say you'd like a quiet little talk together, and I have a score of matters awaiting my attention. Pray excuse me, Phoebe."

Phoebe acceded gracefully, and Lady Denham sailed out of the room.

"Thank goodness!" breathed her daughter, with a grimace. "Mama does go on so, Phoebe — you cannot imagine. And now, tell me of your concerns. Your aunt is with you, is she not? You said she was to arrive yesterday, and you're to go to London. How vastly exciting!"

Phoebe did not look in the least excited, however. "Oh, Nell, I don't wish to go!" she exclaimed in tragic accents. "If only I need not."

"But why? You will have great fun. All those balls and parties, and scores of eligible gentlemen to flirt with."

"Oh, don't," Phoebe said weakly, putting her head in her hands in an attitude of complete despair.

"What have I said now?" demanded Eleanor, a little out of patience with her more emotional friend. "Most girls go into raptures at the thought of such delights — indeed, I wouldn't object to a taste of them myself. Katie has invited me to stay with her in Hanover Square, too, but Mama will not hear of it."

"I only wish my mama were of the same mind," said Phoebe wistfully.

"Come to think of it," remarked Eleanor, her curiosity aroused, "it is unlike Lady Chalgrove to want you to go away from home, even for a short spell. How did that come about? I never thought to ask you before, taking it for granted that you had wheedled her into the scheme — but now, of course, I realise you didn't, as you're so set against going."

Phoebe sighed. "You should know one cannot wheedle Mama into anything, Nell. For a gentle person, she is surprisingly inflexible. It was Lord Ashcroft who first suggested that both Tom and I should have a season in London, as he felt we would benefit from a spell of town life. Mama wouldn't hear of Tom's absenting himself from his estate duties, but she did come round to thinking it a very good notion as far as I'm concerned. I only wish she hadn't." She sighed.

"Wants to see you married, I dare say," said Eleanor bluntly. "All those eligible gentlemen, you know, Phoebe." Her dancing eyes tried to win some light-hearted response from her friend, but failed.

Lady Phoebe sighed again, this time more heavily. "One particular gentleman, I suspect, Nell. Oh, if only she would let me be."

"Truly?" Eleanor's mobile face was alive with curiosity. "Someone in London, I suppose? Do I know the gentleman? Though it's hardly likely that I should."

"I believe you have met him," replied Phoebe, in a lacklustre tone. "That was some time ago, though."

"Well, don't you mean to tell me who it is?" demanded Eleanor impatiently. "Teasing girl!"

"I can't joke about it, Nell. It's all too serious." There was a break in Phoebe's voice. "Mama has said nothing directly to me, of course, but I've good reason to think she wishes me to wed my cousin Frederick."

"Your cousin — good heavens, can you mean Mr. Frederick Eversley?"

Phoebe nodded miserably.

"Oh! Has he already asked permission to pay his addresses?"

This succeeded in shaking Phoebe out of her torpor. "No, no, nothing of that kind. Indeed, my Aunt Eversley gives us to understand that he has no present thought of marriage. I believe Mama thinks that once we are brought together frequently in London —"

"That your beauty may overcome his reluctance," supplied Nell quickly, with a smile. "And I dare say it will, my love, for you must realise you're quite out of the common way, and able to compete with any of the London belles. No need to be missish —" as Phoebe started to disclaim modestly — "for we know each other too well, both good and bad, for any pretence between us. But I must admit," she continued, with a frown, "that it puzzles me to know why Lady Chalgrove should desire you to marry your cousin. It would be a good match, of course, but could hardly be considered a brilliant one, as he is only the youngest son of a viscount, while you are an earl's daughter. Most mothers seem obsessed by considerations of rank in these matters." There was a touch of bitterness in her voice on these final words.

"Well, the Eversley title is of greater antiquity than ours, if Mama were concerned about rank," said Phoebe. "But I'm sure she's not. What she earnestly desires is to keep me within the family circle, close to her, and marriage to Freddy would achieve that, or so she believes. I chanced to overhear her saying so to Lord Ashcroft."

"I wouldn't be so certain. Your cousin seems to me to be possessed of his own notions, in spite of his easy-going manner," retorted Nell, remembering her recent encounter with the Honourable Frederick. "But can this be *all* your mama's reason? It hardly seems enough, unless her sister is equally set on the notion, and each spurs on the other."

"No, I think not. I believe it's all on Mama's part, for I have the impression that my aunt would never interfere in Freddy's concerns. They are an affectionate family, but not so closely involved with each other as ours. You know how it is with Mama," she finished, on a note of desperation.

Having been acquainted with the Chalgroves all her life, Eleanor did indeed know. She nodded. "What is your objection to the scheme, Phoebe?" she asked, in a quizzical tone. "Have you no tender feelings towards your cousin?"

"Oh, no! Not that he isn't an amiable and personable gentleman such as most females would admire," conceded Phoebe, as an afterthought.

Amiable was not the word which Eleanor would have herself applied to the gentleman of her earlier encounter; but she let this pass, allowing that it might in general be a just description. She unfastened the towel from her head and shook loose her drying chestnut curls. "Then there's some other reason. Tell me."

"There is," confessed Phoebe bashfully. "A particular reason for my not feeling attracted to my cousin, or indeed, any other gentleman —" her voice dropped — "except one."

Eleanor looked sharply at her for a moment, then nodded. "Geoffrey Lydhurst," she stated triumphantly.

A most becoming blush suffused Phoebe's delicate cheeks. "I thought you might have guessed. I love him, Nell, and I know he returns my feelings, though nothing has been said. I fear he will never speak, for he realises that Mama would not look with favour on the match. He is too conscious of the fact that a baronet's son cannot hope to win an earl's daughter!" she burst out passionately. "As if I care a groat for that! But Mama does, alas."

"But I thought you said she was indifferent to considerations of rank?" objected Eleanor.

"Only where my cousin's concerned. When I overheard her conversation with Lord Ashcroft — it was quite by chance, Nell, but I could not help but listen when I heard my own name — she said that I could do better for myself than wed a country squire's son. Lord Ashcroft had just mentioned Geoffrey, so there could be no doubt of whom Mama spoke."

"Then we must find a way out of this tangle," said Eleanor decisively. "Wait — let me think."

A look of deep concentration came over her usually lively face, while Phoebe watched, with hope dawning in her eyes. It had always been Nell who had found a way out of their difficulties in the past. She was a girl of infinite resource, even if at times her schemes were too bold for the more prudent, timid Phoebe.

"But of course!" exclaimed Eleanor triumphantly, after a pause of several minutes. "I have it."

Phoebe drew in a deep, somewhat apprehensive breath, anticipating some outrageous suggestion. "Pray do not say we must elope, Nell," she pleaded apologetically. "I couldn't, truly I couldn't, and I'm sure Geoffrey would never consent to it, even if I did."

"Elope?" repeated Nell scornfully. "Goodness, no! I don't believe even I would consider such a course. Not nowadays, though I might have, once. No, the solution I've come upon doesn't violate any code of propriety."

Phoebe's relief was evident. "What is it, dearest Nell?" she breathed.

"Why, simply that you should recommend Geoffrey Lydhurst to address himself to your brother for permission to marry you — that's when you've persuaded him to declare his feelings to you, of course," she added, with a teasing smile.

"To Tom! But —"

"There's no denying the fact, Phoebe, that Tom is the head of the family, and the proper person to whom a suitor for your hand should apply," said Eleanor firmly.

"But Mama would be deeply hurt — indeed, outraged," protested Phoebe. "She considers herself to be my guardian. She would never forgive either of us. Oh no, it's not possible. Besides," she added forlornly, "Tom would never go against Mama."

Eleanor considered this for a moment. She was well aware that Lady Chalgrove still held the reins in that household. It was one more objection she had advanced to her own mother against the felicity of a marriage between herself and the young earl. "Could you not work on Lord Ashcroft to act as mediator on your behalf, Phoebe? I know your mother values his advice, and he is extremely fond of you. He thinks well of Geoffrey, too."

"'Tis of no use, I fear. He was attempting to plead Geoffrey's cause in that conversation I overheard, but Mama would not listen to him. No, Nell, there seems nothing else for me to do than to — to try to forget him —" Her final words were punctuated by sobs.

Nell put a comforting arm about her. "There, there, don't cry, my love. I'll see if I can think of another way. There must be something." She relapsed into thought once again, patting and soothing the grief-stricken Phoebe meanwhile. "Could we perhaps stage some incident in which Lydhurst rescues you from danger?" she wondered, half to herself. "If your mother were to believe that she owed the preservation of your life to him —"

Phoebe raised a tearstained, anxious face. "But I would not at all like to be in any danger!"

"Silly girl, you wouldn't be in any real danger — it would just appear so. Now, what could we arrange, I wonder? One of the difficulties is that you're never allowed out unescorted. Otherwise we could manage some such accident as befell me today, only you could sprain your ankle and lie for hours in a ditch while your family hunted high and low for you — and then, when all hope was lost, Geoffrey Lydhurst would discover you and bring you safely home. There, what do you think of that?"

Even before Phoebe uttered a word in reply, it was obvious from her shocked expression that this ingenious scheme failed utterly to recommend itself to her. She proceeded to enumerate her objections, not least among them her dislike of lying for hours in a ditch with a sprained ankle.

"But of course you wouldn't actually lie in the ditch," insisted Eleanor, somewhat impatiently. "We could choose somewhere with a barn or shed nearby where you could hide away until the time came for Geoffrey to rescue you. I think I know the very place," she went on eagerly. "There is just such a disused, tumbledown shed on Oakland Common."

Phoebe shuddered. "I expect it is covered in cobwebs and there'll be black beetles and mice. Oh no, Nell, I couldn't! And then, a sprained ankle —"

"Pooh!" exclaimed Eleanor scornfully. "Anyone can pretend to have sprained an ankle — nothing easier. You have only to limp and screw up your face in pain. It is all to be playacting, don't you see, Phoebe? Of course, Lydhurst would have to be in on the secret."

"Never!" declared Phoebe, with unaccustomed firmness. "What must he think of me, were I to suggest such a — I'm sorry, Nell, but I can call it none other than a wild scheme, involving us both in a tissue of lies. No, it isn't possible."

"Very well," replied Eleanor, with an affronted expression. "If you're to be so poor-spirited, I don't see how I am to help you."

Phoebe laid a hand on her arm with a pleading gesture. "Pray don't be vexed with me, dear Nell, for I do appreciate your efforts to assist. You are the kindest and best of good friends. But I'm not nearly as adventurous as you, and solutions which seem possible to you are, I fear, quite beyond my scope." She sighed. "I see I must reconcile myself for the present, and trust to time to arrange matters. Most likely my cousin will never show any more interest in me than he does at present, even when we are constantly brought together in London, as we are certain to be. And then Mama will be obliged to give up her scheme."

"Does he really appear indifferent to you?" asked Eleanor, surprised, for Phoebe's exceptional beauty dazzled most males who came into contact with her.

Phoebe laughed. "Oh, completely! Except as a family connection, of course."

Eleanor felt ready to accept this assurance, for even such a modest girl as her friend could not fail to be aware of a gentleman's admiration. She pondered once more, then gave a triumphant exclamation as she turned a radiant face towards Phoebe. "I have it! I've thought of the perfect plan to make your mama abandon her matchmaking. And the best of it is that it won't require any action on your part, nor on Lydhurst's, either — at least, not yet. Now, do you think you could invite me to dine with your family this evening?"

The two girls did occasionally spend an evening in each other's homes in this way, but Lady Chalgrove preferred to be consulted in advance before an invitation was issued. Phoebe's assent was therefore somewhat guarded.

"Make some excuse," Eleanor urged her, at once understanding her friend's hesitation. "Say that my parents are dining out this evening — that is true, by the way — and I asked you to come here, but you felt you could not because you have guests at home. So you invited me, instead. What could be more natural than that, I ask you?"

Phoebe's brow cleared. "Yes, I think that will be all right. But what is this plan of yours, Nell? Do tell me."

Eleanor laughed. "No, for you might spoil it inadvertently, if you knew. You must wait and see, my love."

CHAPTER IV

As Frederick Eversley was changing his clothes for dinner that evening, he reflected that the day had not gone off so badly as he had feared.

His encounter with the bedraggled Miss Denham that morning had afforded him a good deal of quiet amusement. It seemed that she had not changed much over the years from the harum-scarum girl he remembered at Brighton, in spite of the dignified airs she had assumed when he was escorting her home. He had said nothing of the incident to Tom when they met later, for they had both been too taken up with a visit to the stables and an animated discussion on horseflesh; but sometime or other, he must mention Miss Denham, and see what his cousin thought of the young lady. As a near neighbour, she must be well known to the Chalgroves.

What he was not at all prepared for was to find her sitting in the drawing room with the other ladies of his family when he finally presented himself there. Indeed, at first he failed to recognise her, which was scarcely surprising. The slim, shapely young lady, in a fashionable gown of diaphanous white muslin worn over an apricot silk petticoat, with her chestnut curls burnished and glowing, bore no resemblance whatever to the mud-spattered scarecrow of their earlier meeting.

He was introduced, but before he could bow in response, she had risen impetuously and stretched out her hands towards him, forcing him to take them in his.

"But Mr. Eversley and I are old acquaintances!" she exclaimed, with an unexpectedly warm glance at him from her lively hazel eyes. "We met two years ago in Brighton — shall I ever forget?"

Her pronouncement, and more particularly the manner of it, produced all the effect on the rest of the company that she could possibly have desired. Lady Chalgrove looked scandalised, Phoebe choked, and her brother glared; Lady Eversley raised her brows. The Honourable Frederick looked first surprised, then amused.

"Just so, ma'am," he agreed equably, releasing her hands quickly and bowing.

"And we met more recently," she went on, in a stage whisper over his bowed head. "Or am I being indiscreet in saying so?"

Tom's brow became thunderous. Freddy withdrew calmly, having made no reply to this. It was fortunate that at the same moment dinner was announced. They all moved into the dining-room, each of the gentlemen taking one of the older ladies on his arm, while Phoebe and Eleanor walked in together.

"Nell, what on earth are you up to?" demanded Phoebe, in an agonised whisper.

"Hush, you'll see. There's more to come," promised Eleanor, with a wicked smile.

There was no time to say anything further, but Phoebe began to fear that it would not be a comfortable evening.

The feeling grew as the meal progressed. Lady Chalgrove had arranged her table as best she might with only two gentlemen to four ladies. She placed Tom, of course, at the head, with Lady Eversley on his right and Phoebe on his left. Next to Phoebe was her cousin Frederick, while Lady Chalgrove sat at the end with Eleanor on her left, next to Lady Eversley.

At first she was satisfied with this arrangement, for whenever the conversation was not general, Frederick chatted to Phoebe

— which was just what Lady Chalgrove had hoped for — while Eleanor talked to Lady Eversley, who was acquainted with Eleanor's sister in London, Catherine Pamyngton. Lady Chalgrove's chief object in her seating plan had been to place Miss Denham as far away from Tom as possible. She had certainly not foreseen any possible undesirable consequences in having the wretched girl opposite Frederick.

But so it proved. Having chatted for a while to Lady Eversley, Eleanor turned her attention to Frederick, favouring him with a brilliant coy smile as she asked if he did not recall what fun they had both enjoyed together two years before in Brighton.

The intimate tone in which she put the question, coupled with the enthusiastic welcome she had accorded him earlier, puzzled him a good deal after her coldness during their morning encounter, but he did not allow this sentiment to show. Females were changeable creatures, after all, he told himself, and there was no denying that the girl was very attractive in her present mood.

He returned her smile. "Oh, Brighton's undoubtedly the place for fun, Miss Denham," he answered lightly.

"Yes, but I was thinking more particularly," she continued, with a saucy gleam in her hazel eyes, "of the fun you and I had together, just the two of us, at White Hawk fair. I so much wished to go, but the rest of our party wouldn't agree, and then you said you would accompany me — don't you remember? So we rode off, and left them behind."

Freddy saw that all conversation at the table had been suspended, and the others were regarding him with various expressions, none of which could be deemed approving. His cravat began to feel too tight. "I do recall something of the kind," he said coolly. "I rather think your sister and Pamyngton followed us, though."

"Oh, but that was not for some time afterwards," she corrected him, with another intimate look. "We were quite alone when we visited the fortune teller. She told me to beware of a personable gentleman who would try to lead me astray, you may recollect! I cannot imagine whom she might have meant, can you?" Receiving no response to this leading question beyond a slightly embarrassed smile, she plunged on, listened to by a stunned audience. "And then we went on the merry-go-round," she continued. "I did so enjoy it, what with your making me laugh all the time with the most absurd quips. It was a pity that it ended in a mishap, though I didn't care a jot about my ricked ankle, I assure you. You held out your arms for me to jump into when the machine stopped, but I foolishly misjudged the distance."

The Honourable Frederick could never so far forget himself as to contradict a lady in public, but his recollection of this incident differed from Miss Denham's. He had certainly offered her a helping hand to dismount, but she had spurned his aid and jumped recklessly from her wooden horse, turning her ankle as she landed. To say that he had held out his arms to her was, he thought indignantly, an exaggeration. He began to wonder what this attractive little minx was about, and determined not to let her have things all her own way. "Ah, well, our salad days, what, ma'am?" he said lightly. "Dare say you prefer to forget them."

"Forget them? Never!" she exclaimed, her eyes big with reproach. "And surely you haven't forgotten that once you offered to slay dragons for me, or fetch treasure from the ends of the earth, if by so doing you might earn my friendship?"

There was an outraged gasp from Tom, but the rest of the diners preserved a frozen silence.

Frederick's eye now had a steely glint in it, but he kept his tone light. "Can't say I recall that, Miss Denham, but I dare say we were both in a frivolous mood at the time."

"*Frivolous?*" she echoed, and he noticed with disgust that the audacious chit's lip was actually quivering. "Oh, and I thought you serious!"

To her chagrin, he laughed. "Splendid, ma'am!" he applauded. "You are a born actress. Do you ever take part in amateur theatricals? They're all the rage nowadays."

For a moment, she looked disconcerted, and he thought he had succeeded in putting an end to whatever charade she was playing. She rallied, however, with what was a most unexpected thrust. "How could you?" she whispered in a broken voice which nevertheless carried clearly to the ears of all present. "And after our meeting this morning, too!"

At this, Tom was starting to his feet, but his sister laid a restraining hand on his arm. At the same moment, Lady Chalgrove indicated in icy accents that it was time for the ladies to retire and leave the gentlemen with their wine.

Barely had the door closed behind the females of the party than Tom strode towards his cousin, a murderous look on his face. "By heaven, Frederick, you'll answer to me for this!" he exploded. "'Tis plain you've been playing fast and loose with Miss Denham's affections. The poor girl may not have a brother to call you to account, but I'll do so, you villain."

"Oh, calm down, you cloth-head," retorted Freddy. "Can't you see the girl was playacting for some obscure reason of her own?"

"Yes, so you tried to say, but that didn't take me in. You'll give me satisfaction for this!"

"What, are you proposing a *duel?*" demanded Freddy, with an incredulous laugh. "Let me tell you they're considered very bad form nowadays. Besides, how can I possibly fight a member of my own family? Not to mention the scandal there'd be. It would do the girl more harm than good, if you think about it. Take a glass of wine, old fellow, and let's discuss the matter sensibly."

"Take a glass of wine with you?" said Tom, between set teeth. "I'd as soon throw it in your face, you — you deceiver of innocent females!"

Freddy shrugged. "Please yourself," he said, sitting down again and reaching for the decanter, "but I mean to take wine in the more normal way. And I don't mind telling you, Tom, that if you persist in talking in that dramatic style, I shall think you ought to join Miss Denham in gracing the boards."

His bantering tone succeeded in making the young earl feel foolish, and somewhat abated his wrath. After all, he had always considered his cousin to be the best of good fellows, for he had frequently had cause to be grateful to Freddy during their schooldays.

"I'd like to plant you a facer," he said, but in a less belligerent tone.

"Oh, I'll provide that kind of satisfaction if you wish," replied Freddy, filling his glass, "but not here and now, do you think? Mustn't upset the ladies. I may as well warn you, though, that I spend some of my time at Gentleman Jackson's boxing saloon when I'm in town."

"Do you think I'm afraid of you?" sneered his cousin.

"Certainly not, old chap. Oh, for heaven's sake, take that melodramatic look off your face, and sit down. Here, I'll fill your glass."

Tom subsided reluctantly into a chair, his anger rapidly cooling, and took the proffered wine. "All the same, you'll need to explain yourself," he said determinedly. "Miss Denham can't have spoken in the way she did without good cause, I'll warrant."

"No," replied Freddy, in a considering tone. "Now, I wonder just what the cause might have been? By the way, Tom, why are you so hot in the lady's defence?"

"Because," said Tom, defiantly, "she is the lady I am thinking of making my wife."

"I see. Have you declared yourself? You've said nothing to me so far of an engagement."

Tom looked a little crestfallen. "Well, no. The thing is, you see, that my mother doesn't favour Miss Denham. Naturally, I don't care to go against Mama."

Freddy nodded, well aware of this fact. "Would you say the lady herself appears agreeable to receiving your addresses?" he asked.

Tom flushed. "I don't know. We've been acquainted all our lives, and deal extremely well together."

"I rather fancy," said Freddy carefully, "that she's not the first girl you've had your eye upon?"

Tom flushed. "Well, no — you know how it is — only natural for a man to look about him. Not that there are so many to choose from, around these parts. But this time I'm serious," he finished defiantly.

"Just so. But I'd have thought you're a trifle young to be dashing into parson's mousetrap. I mean to avoid that fate myself for several years yet. There's a deal to be said for a bachelor existence."

"So there may be in London," said Tom enviously. "It's a different matter here, with Mama keeping my nose to the grindstone as far as the estate's concerned, and not choosing for us to mix freely with all our neighbours. She says I'm too young for marriage."

"Does she, indeed? Well, for once my aunt and I are in agreement. Tell you what, Tom, why don't you come back to town with us for a spell? Shake a loose leg for a few months, what?"

This was a truly noble offer on Freddy's part, for he had no desire to be forced yet again into the role of guardian to his cousin, which he had played during their schooldays. He was too good-natured not to feel sorry, however, for a young man of Tom's age who was still, to all intents and purposes, in leading strings.

Tom's face took on a despondent look. "It's of no use, Freddy! Ashcroft, my godfather, you know, tried to persuade her, and though she listens to him more than anyone, he didn't succeed."

"Shall I have a go at it? Not that I think I'm exactly popular with my Aunt Ianthe."

"Oh, would you? She likes you, Freddy. I heard her praising you up to Phoebe before you arrived. And she might find it difficult to refuse a definite invitation from you."

This Frederick found hard to credit, but he agreed to make the attempt.

"You're a right 'un," pronounced Tom, much cheered by this promise. He poured a second glass of wine for them both, then belatedly remembered that the most important part of their conversation had been shelved, whether deliberately or not, he could not be sure. "But you still haven't explained Miss Denham's remarks," he challenged.

"That's because I can't — at least, I can't tell you why she chose to put such a riotous interpretation upon what were completely commonplace events," replied his cousin. "I assure you, Tom, that the only time I was ever alone with the girl during that sojourn in Brighton was for a bare half-hour or so in a crowded fairground. She was only just out of the schoolroom then, and up to all manner of games, like any spirited chit of that age. Nothing would do for her but to ride on the merry-go-round, and I thought it a prime lark myself, but I can promise you that I decidedly did not hold out my arms for her to jump into them. She jumped off before I could assist her, and as a result the wretched — that's to say, she hurt her ankle. Yes, and the to-do there was over that, with everyone crowding to help, and her sister exclaiming over her. I can tell you, I wished myself elsewhere. Wished, too, I'd had the gumption to stop her from going on the contraption in the first place. Not that I think anyone could stop that young lady from doing anything she'd a mind to." Just in time he restrained himself from describing Miss Denham as a rackety female with more hair than wit.

Tom nodded. "Yes, she has a deal of spirit," he agreed fondly. "But what about your saying you'd slay dragons and so on, to earn her friendship? If that doesn't sound like flirting, tell me what does?"

"I can't recall that, but take it from me it's all a lie. I was never alone with the girl on any other occasion than the fairground episode, so whatever nonsense may have passed between us was spoken in the full hearing of the rest of the company. Besides, do you seriously suppose I'd flirt with a schoolgirl to the extent of making her think me serious? I may enjoy a flirtation now and then with a female who perfectly understands the game, but I'm not such a rum touch as that," concluded Freddy, in a hurt tone.

"No," answered Tom, wrinkling his brow. "No, I don't think you are. What was that, though, about a meeting this morning? I must say, Freddy —"

"Then you may as well restrain yourself," interrupted his cousin promptly, "for I can recount the whole of that episode to you, chapter and verse." He proceeded to do so, finding a certain amount of entertainment in the other's increasingly bewildered expression.

"But I don't at all understand," complained Tom, in a puzzled tone. "If you met quite by accident, and she was in a miff with you all the time — which I'm bound to say she would be if you were so foolhardy as to suggest she couldn't manage her mare — then why did she speak as though it had been a clandestine meeting? It doesn't make sense to me."

It was beginning to make sense to Frederick, however, though the conclusions at which he was arriving were not such as he wished to share with his cousin. He fancied he could hazard a guess at the lady's game, and his face hardened. "No accounting for females," he said, with a shrug. "As long as you and I don't come to blows over it, there's no harm in whatever game the lady's playing. Shall we adjourn to the drawing-room?"

As Eleanor accompanied the other ladies to the drawing-room, she silently congratulated herself on having made some headway in her plan to assist Phoebe. It was surprising how easy it was to mislead people without actually resorting to untruths, she reflected. Her account of the episodes with Mr. Eversley at Brighton had been factually accurate, but the exaggerated light in which she had represented them had succeeded in conveying a totally false impression to her hearers. She felt confident that everyone except his mother, who would know him better, must now be judging Mr. Eversley as an unscrupulous flirt who had toyed with the affections of a young and innocent girl. As a result, Lady Chalgrove would undoubtedly be repenting of her matchmaking scheme. So far, so good, thought Eleanor.

She was not without some qualms of conscience, however, on Frederick Eversley's account. From what she knew of him, she did not consider him at all capable of acting the shabby part in which she had cast him. Still, it could do him no lasting harm. He was not in love with Phoebe, and had he been aware of his aunt's plan to make a match between them, most likely he would even have felt grateful. Besides, thought Eleanor indignantly, he deserved paying back for his high-handed treatment of her that morning.

Phoebe gave her a puzzled look as they all left the dining-room, and Eleanor wondered how well her friend had understood the purpose behind that flood of tender reminiscence. She would have liked to explain, but any private conversation between them was quite impossible at present. The best she could do was to give Phoebe a glance charged with significance.

Once seated in the elegant drawing-room, a constraint fell over the party. Lady Eversley, always the soul of tact, attempted to dispel this by launching tirelessly into a painstaking account of the latest London fashions, the only safe topic that came to mind. Eleanor soon joined in, quoting from her sister Catherine's letters on that subject. A surreptitious nudge to Phoebe persuaded her to try and contribute an occasional remark. Only Lady Chalgrove remained aloof, surveying Eleanor from time to time with a look of cold disdain which would have totally unnerved a more timid female.

But Eleanor refused to be daunted. She was well aware that she had never been a favourite with her hostess, and that she might find herself even less welcome at Chalgrove Park in future. No matter for that, she thought; Phoebe would be absent from home for several months, and it was to see Phoebe that she came. As for Tom, he could always seek her out if he wished.

She was somewhat piqued to observe, when the gentlemen entered the room, that Mr. Eversley gave her a cool amused glance before going to sit beside Phoebe. He seemed not at all embarrassed by her revelations at the dining-table, and quite evidently, she thought disgustedly, had set her down as a foolish female with a taste for melodrama.

Fortunately for her peace of mind, it never occurred to her that both Mr. Eversley and Lady Chalgrove had arrived independently at the same explanation for her behaviour, and, moreover, one very far removed from the truth. It was unfortunately confirmed in Lady Chalgrove's mind when she saw her son go straight to Eleanor's side on entering the room, with every appearance of intending to remain there for the duration of the evening. At all costs, she thought desperately, Tom had to be removed from the influence of this scheming creature before matters got out of hand.

It was certainly not a comfortable evening. Eleanor would have liked to pursue her purpose of presenting the unlucky Mr. Eversley in an unattractive guise to her hostess, but no further opportunity offered itself. For some time Tom remained at her side, talking animatedly about tomorrow's hunt, while the rest of the party engaged in desultory conversation. Then Lady Eversley hit upon the happy notion of a musical interlude, thinking that this would preclude conversation and so do away with the strain of finding safe topics.

The ruse answered tolerably well. Eleanor and Phoebe were induced to oblige, and both moved over to the pianoforte at the other side of the room in order to select some suitable pieces. With their heads close together over the sheets of music, Eleanor managed to whisper a quick explanation to her friend.

"But was it true, what you said?" whispered back Phoebe. "Did he really behave so shamefully?"

"No, but I can't tell you now — another time. Look, your mama's eye is upon us, so you'd better play this Mozart sonatina."

Phoebe obediently sat down at the pianoforte and a respectful silence fell over the seemingly attentive audience, most of whom, however, were engaged with their private thoughts. When she rose to polite applause, Eleanor dutifully took her place. After that, it was time for the tea tray to be brought in, and soon Eleanor's carriage was at the door to convey her home.

After she had gone, Tom and Freddy repaired once more to the billiard-room and Phoebe excused herself to her elders, saying she wished to retire.

"Well!" declared Lady Chalgrove, once she and her sister were alone. "I suppose you can't wonder now that I was far from pleased when Phoebe told me she'd invited that female to dine with us. Did you ever see such a forward minx? I don't need to tell you that I didn't believe a word of what she insinuated about Frederick's behaviour. It is all too plain what she was about."

"Aren't you being a little severe on her, Ianthe? Of course, she's a lively girl, like her sister young Lady Pamyngton, whom I'm forever meeting in town."

"Severe? I wonder you should say so, when it was your own son she was maligning!"

Lady Eversley chuckled. "Well, as to that, I think Freddy paid her out in her own coin. But when you've had two such harum-scarum daughters as my Evelina and Georgiana, you cease to be surprised at anything girls may do. Of course, your Phoebe is a model of propriety, so you're not as accustomed as I am to freakish starts. But what do you mean when you say you knew what she was about? Wasn't it simply to make Freddy appear as a rake, or something of that kind? Absurd!" She chuckled again.

"I'm glad you find it amusing," replied her sister coldly. "However, if you're not concerned on your own son's account, I certainly am on mine. Eleanor Denham deliberately created the impression that there had been a connection of an amorous kind between herself and Frederick in order, I am certain, to bring on Tom's addresses! You see, he has been interested in her all this winter, and her mother is naturally anxious to see her make such a brilliant match. There's nothing like the hint of a rival to bring a man to the point, as we both know. Oh, yes, the girl is fiendishly clever, but she shan't lure him into her trap, if I can do anything to prevent it. I wasn't in favour of his going to town when first you suggested he might accompany Phoebe, but now I would be glad to accept on his behalf, if your kind invitation still holds."

"But of course we shall be delighted to have him stay with us," replied Lady Eversley warmly. "That is, if he wishes to do so."

"Oh, he's been anxious to go up to town for ages. He's forever suggesting that we should take a house there for the season, but I have remained firm on that subject. If the duties of a large estate are to be discharged conscientiously, the landowner must be on hand."

"But not all the time, surely, Ianthe? That is to be a prisoner in one's own home," protested Lady Eversley.

Her sister's lips set in an obstinate line. "You must allow me to know my own business best, Anne," she said. "However, as matters stand at present with the Denham girl, I consider a short absence from home would be advisable for Thomas. And under your husband's guidance, I am sure he can come to no harm in London."

Thus it was that Freddy found his application to his aunt on Tom's behalf was granted with a readiness which surprised both young men.

CHAPTER V

The following day, Freddy and Tom rode out together to join the hunt, the only activity for which Freddy had been able to raise any enthusiasm since arriving at Chalgrove Park. The meet was at Lydhurst Manor, for Sir Bertram Lydhurst was Master of Foxhounds, following the practice of his family for generations. Geoffrey Lydhurst, a dark-haired young man of Tom's age with a pleasant, open countenance and a broad-shouldered, athletic figure, greeted the newcomers warmly.

"A good day for it, Tom — just a hint of moisture in the air, but no fear of rain, we think. Glad to see you with us, Eversley. It's some time since we last met. I dare say you don't get the chance to follow the hounds very often. I trust we'll show you a good day's sport."

Frederick replied suitably, and Sir Bertram joined them briefly for a word before passing among the other assembled riders. Several of these were ladies of various ages, and among them was Eleanor Denham, he noticed, looking very dashing in a habit of mulberry cloth, a muslin cravat and a tall crowned hat with a plume of ostrich feathers. She was mounted on that same high-couraged chestnut which he had presumed to suggest was an unsuitable mount for a lady. He could not help reflecting on the very different figure she had presented yesterday after her tumble in the ditch, and a broad grin spread over his face at this recollection. She chanced to look in his direction at that moment, and seemed to understand his expression, for she rewarded him with a slight, unsmiling inclination of the head. He returned the bow, but refrained from joining Tom when the latter went quickly towards her group. He had already promised himself an interview with the lady before he returned to town, but this was obviously neither the time nor the place for it.

The hounds came out, and the party moved off to the first covert, Freddy riding alongside Geoffrey Lydhurst and Lord Ashcroft, who never missed a meet.

"Pity little Phoebe takes no pleasure in the sport," remarked Ashcroft. "Quite a few females here, though. Must say it does me good to see Nell Denham riding so fearlessly in the field. She's a more robust girl than Phoebe, of course."

"Yes, indeed," agreed Lydhurst, obviously thinking that the word robust could certainly not apply to such an ethereal being as Lady Phoebe. "My sister Meg has no liking for following the hounds, either, so they're to spend the morning together at home. There's to be an impromptu party with dancing — couldn't really call it a ball, just a few hunt members and other neighbours — at the manor this evening. Eversley, may we hope to see you there with Tom and his sister?"

Freddy accepted this invitation readily, grateful for the prospect of an evening spent away from his aunt's fireside.

During the course of the rousing morning's sport that followed, he caught occasional glimpses of Miss Denham, and had to acknowledge that he had been quite out in his judgment that her mare was too much of a handful for her. She careered across the fields, clearing hedges and ditches faultlessly and leaving several of the male riders behind. Without doubt, the girl's horsemanship was all that she had claimed.

Later that day, Freddy joined a party of some twenty couples, mostly young people, in the long room at Lydhurst Manor which had been added to the original Tudor building for assemblies of this kind. His infrequent visits to the neighbourhood meant that he was not previously acquainted with many of those present, but his easy address soon recommended him to everybody. Among most of the young ladies, he created a stir of interest as being an unattached, personable gentleman with that unmistakable London polish to which all young people aspired.

It was not long before the dancing began — an informal business with only a pianoforte accompaniment, and small ceremony in the selection of partners. Tom would have led out Eleanor far more frequently than she would permit, but she had no intention of allowing his interest in her to show, even in such a free and easy setting. She was looking especially charming in a high-waisted gown of white gauze over a slip of aquamarine satin, with her chestnut curls piled high on her head and confined by a ribbon of the same shade. She had no lack of partners, so Freddy bided his time before approaching her when Tom was doing his duty by his host's daughter, Margaret Lydhurst.

Freddy neatly intercepted a young dandy who was about to lead Eleanor out, and bowed before her. "Our dance, I believe, Miss Denham," he said.

She gave him a slightly flustered look. She had been trying to avoid him all day, only too conscious of her behaviour of the previous evening, and the probable effect this had had upon him. "Oh, there's no formality here, sir," she replied, with an attempt at a careless shrug. "One doesn't engage oneself to any particular partner, you know."

"Ah, but you and I, ma'am," he replied, with a meaning look, "share an intimate past, do we not? I've waited patiently all evening for the opportunity to renew that warm friendship of which you spoke so feelingly last night."

A fiery blush greeted this sally, and she was for the moment too discomposed to prevent him from taking her limp hand and leading her into the set that was forming.

"I must confess," he went on, enjoying her momentary confusion, "that I was both surprised — and, of course, flattered — that you should have recalled any words of mine after such a long interval. I scarcely dared to hope that you have any clear remembrance of their unworthy speaker."

"Mr. Eversley, I must tell you that —" she paused, and swallowed — "what I said was nonsensical, and I beg you will forget it."

"Forget it? Oh, never!" he declaimed, in a melodramatic tone to match the one she had adopted at the Eversleys' manor. "What man who has been so honoured —"

She gritted her teeth. "I know you are quizzing me," she said, in an angry tone, "and I suppose in some way I may deserve it. But pray don't — there was a very good reason why I spoke as I did." She paused again, faced with the impossibility of explaining this reason to him.

"Oh, so I supposed," he answered coolly. "I'm not quite such a coxcomb as to imagine that even a young lady straight from the schoolroom, as you were when we met two years ago, would have formed a lasting passion for me on the strength of the insignificant exchanges of common civility which passed between us at that time. Confess it, you were roasting me either to satisfy some inborn love of melodrama, or to pay off the score of my offence in daring to suggest that your mare was a trifle above your touch."

"I certainly did feel vexed with you over that!" she retorted hotly. "And not, I consider, without cause. Your whole manner was high-handed in the extreme."

He reflected on how well she looked when her hazel eyes flashed in that way. "But that wasn't all of it, was it, ma'am? I fancy you had another — and stronger — reason."

She looked at him in a perplexed way. Could he possibly have guessed her intention? She did not know him well, but she judged him to be more astute than his cousin Thomas. On the other hand, it seemed highly unlikely that he would be aware of his aunt's scheme to make a match between himself and Phoebe. "I have already admitted as much to you, sir," she said guardedly. "Is it possible — can you have guessed what that reason was?" She was somewhat taken aback by the steely look which came over his usually pleasant countenance.

"I think so," he said curtly.

They were parted for a few moments by the movements of the dance. Eleanor could scarcely wait for the opportunity to resume their conversation.

"Then, if so, you'll see why I was obliged to exaggerate somewhat, to — to represent your conduct as quite other than in fact it had been." She looked at him apologetically. "I am sorry for it, and freely admit it was a wretched thing to do. But, you see, I could think of nothing else that would work."

He half bowed, ironically. "By all means feel at liberty to make me the humble means to achieve whatever ends you desire."

She coloured. "I can see you do not like it and, indeed, I cannot blame you. But the case was desperate, you know, and I had to do something to help matters along."

"All's fair in love and war, what? Well, Miss Denham, I hope your schemes achieve the result for which you have put forth so much endeavour."

She could make very little of this, delivered as it was in a mocking tone. But there was no further opportunity for conversation during the rest of the dance, and at its conclusion he bowed and relinquished her to another eager partner.

Amid the general gaiety and laughter, two of those present at the party failed to take much pleasure in the proceedings. Phoebe and Geoffrey Lydhurst had danced with several different partners, but only once together, and on that solitary occasion each found the strain almost too much to bear. The thought of their impending separation and its implications weighed heavily on their minds, rendering conversation between them stilted and unnatural. Fortunately, the rest of the company were enjoying themselves too wholeheartedly to have time to observe that these two, who had known each other from childhood, were now conducting themselves like strangers.

After their dance was over, Phoebe, unable to support her spirits without a few moments of solitude, slipped quietly away into a side room which was at present deserted. Lydhurst saw her go and, after a brief inward struggle, followed her unobtrusively.

He found her sitting dejectedly upon a small sofa behind the partly-open door. She started and looked up at his approach, and he saw her lovely blue eyes were misty with tears.

"Phoebe," he said, in a strangled voice. "What is it? Are you unwell?"

She dabbed her eyes with a handkerchief. "It was so hot and noisy in there," she replied, in a shaky tone, "and I wanted to be alone for a while."

"Would you rather I went away?" he asked uncertainly. "Shall I send my sister to you?"

She shook her head, the tears starting again. "No, it's just that — oh, Geoffrey, I wish I were not obliged to go to London!"

He stood looking down at her, fighting a strong impulse to take her in his arms. When he spoke, he did his best to make his tone calm and matter-of-fact. "I dare say you'll like it well enough when you get there. Most girls seem keen for the chance of a London season."

"I am not. I'd much prefer to remain here," she said wistfully.

"Then can you not persuade Lady Chalgrove to allow you to stay?"

She shook her head once more. "It's useless. I've tried, but Mama is quite determined. She — there are reasons why she wishes me to go."

Involuntarily, Lydhurst clenched his hands. "Yes, I dare say I can hazard a guess at them," he said bitterly. "She intends you to make a brilliant match, I don't doubt."

"I don't want a brilliant match!" exclaimed Phoebe passionately. "I want —"

He started towards her, then checked himself with an effort. She looked up at him, and in that moment all the suppressed longing between them showed plainly in their eyes.

"Oh, Phoebe, Phoebe!" he said brokenly. "If only — but what can it matter whether you go or stay?" he finished, in a bitter tone. "Either way, it can make no difference."

"You mean you don't mind?" Her voice was almost suspended by tears.

"*Mind!*" he echoed. "Good heavens, Phoebe, how can you think that? You must know —" He broke off abruptly, biting back the words which he knew should never be spoken.

For a few moments there was silence in the room, while each struggled for composure.

Then he half-turned away from her, unable to bear the sight of her sad little face. "If things were different — if Lady Chalgrove were at all disposed to consider an application from me — but I know only too well that she has higher aspirations for you. She's made that plain enough — oh, Phoebe!" He turned towards her again, avoiding her eyes. "Forgive me," he said in a strained voice. "I shouldn't have spoken. I know I have no right. You will forget. You're young, and so far have met very few men. In London, there'll be no lack of suitors whom Lady Chalgrove will consider eligible, and among them doubtless there'll be one whom you —" Despite the iron control he was exercising over his feelings, at this point he could not continue.

Phoebe rose to her feet, extending a trembling hand towards him. "Never!" she said, in a voice tremulous with emotion. "There can never be anyone else for me."

"Phoebe, I never dared hope —" He took her outstretched hand and carried it to his lips. Then, all else forgotten, he swept her into his arms.

"What the devil —?" demanded an outraged voice.

They started apart and turned to face Tom, who had just come into the room. Closing the door with a snap, he rounded fiercely upon Lydhurst.

"What's the meaning of this? How dare you make so free with my sister? And you, Phoebe, are you lost to all sense of propriety?"

"Not another word to your sister," interrupted Lydhurst quietly. "You must know she is blameless. As for me, you can acquit me of light dalliance. You should know me better. I honour and respect your sister, and for long enough have wished to make her my wife. I would have sought permission to address her, but I realised it was useless. I meant to keep silent, but — deuce take it, Tom," he burst out, "a man can only stand so much! I found her here, unhappy at being sent off to London, and, well, matters came to a head, that's all."

"Heavens above!" muttered Tom, his anger fading. "Not that I didn't suspect —" He turned to his sister. "And you, Phoebe, do you return Geoffrey's regard?"

She nodded, unable to speak for the moment.

"It's the devil of a problem," went on Tom gloomily. "Not that I've any objection myself, but my mother —"

"I know," said Phoebe tearfully, "she'll never give her consent. She wants me to go to London." She buried her face in a handkerchief while both men looked on with the helplessness of males in the presence of a female in tears.

"Oh, for pity's sake, don't cry," adjured Tom with brotherly impatience. "It can solve nothing, and you'll only make yourself look a wreck. I don't see what's to be done."

"Do you think there's any chance I might win over Lady Chalgrove?" asked Lydhurst, who was longing to comfort his love, and considered Tom's treatment of her outrageous. "If you have no objection."

"Well, of course I haven't," replied Tom, with a worried frown. "How should I, seeing as we've known each other since we were both in short coats, and always the best of friends? As a matter of fact, there's no one I'd rather have as a brother-in-law. But my mother — well, that's another matter entirely. She has her own plans for Phoebe, and she doesn't like having her plans upset. But I don't need to tell you that," he added.

"But, Tom," put in Phoebe, who had rallied surprisingly under her brother's cold douche of common sense, "Nell says that you are the head of the house, and Mama must agree to your wishes."

"Nell? Do you mean Eleanor Denham? Well, what has she to do with this?"

"I confided in her," admitted Phoebe shyly, "and she said that you were my legal guardian, and could give me permission to marry whom I pleased."

In spite of his avowed affection for Miss Denham, Tom could not help feeling a little aggrieved with that young lady. "That's all very well," he said morosely, "and, of course, in a way 'tis true enough. But you know as well as I do, Phoebe, that Mama doesn't see matters in that light. As for opposing her — no, I can't do it, not even for you!"

There was a moment's silence during which Phoebe struggled to avoid again bursting into tears, and Lydhurst pondered despairingly.

"Tell you what, though," resumed Tom, in a brighter tone, as a sudden thought struck him. "If you go off to town just as she wishes, but then come back without having made this brilliant match on which she's set her heart, things might be different. She might be glad enough to settle for Geoffrey — not that I mean, old fellow —" turning apologetically to his friend —

71

"that you aren't as good as any of them. I'm putting it badly, but you know what I mean."

Lydhurst gave an austere smile. "Don't concern yourself, I do know. But it isn't possible to suppose that a young lady of such beauty and charm —" he gave Phoebe a tender look which she returned with a tremulous smile — "won't be at once besieged by scores of eligible suitors in London."

"But if she won't have any of them, even my mother can't force her to the altar," protested Tom. "Besides," he added, on a second bright thought, "I shall be there, shan't I? And, as Nell Denham says, I am Phoebe's guardian, so they'll apply to me for permission to address her. If I refuse them, that's the end of the business."

"Are you to go to London?" asked Lydhurst in amazement. "But I understood that you'd been unable to prevail upon Lady Chalgrove to let you go. You told me so only the other day."

"So I did, but she's relented since then. My cousin Eversley, good fellow, managed to persuade her that I could be spared for a month or so. Well, that's all settled then, isn't it? I think we'd best return to the others before we're missed."

He felt very pleased with himself at having successfully postponed an awkward decision on such a delicate matter, for it was the young earl's habit to avoid anything that threatened unpleasantness. The two who followed him back into the ballroom, however, felt no such gratification. Lydhurst had the uneasy conviction that Lady Chalgrove's sister would acquaint her with all the details of Phoebe's conquests, so that Tom's summary dismissal of her suitors would count for nothing. Phoebe, knowing exactly what her mother intended, but too shy to reveal this to either of her companions, could only hope desperately that Nell's efforts to discredit Frederick Eversley in her mama's eyes had not been without success.

Although it was generally known in the neighbourhood that Lady Phoebe Chalgrove was to have a season in London with her aunt, the news of her brother's imminent departure had not had time to circulate. Had it not been for a chance meeting the next day between Lord Ashcroft and Sir George Denham, Lady Denham would have been as ignorant of this fact as everyone else; but her spouse, knowing her keen interest in the young earl, informed her as soon as he returned home.

"He's going up to town for some time," she repeated in dismay. "Could anything be more unfortunate?"

"I don't see that, my dear. It'll be a splendid thing for the young fellow to break loose from his mother's apron strings. I agree with Ashcroft over that. It will make a man of him."

"Why must you pretend to be so stupid, Denham?" she demanded, exasperated. "You know well enough that I am thinking of Eleanor's interests."

"Oh, I know you've got your eye on him for Nell, but I'm not so sure, myself. I don't see any signs in the girl of a particular interest in Chalgrove. She flirts with him a bit, of course, but that's only natural in a high-spirited chit like Nell." He chuckled.

"That's not the point," she snapped. "He has been paying her particular attention of late, and if they're to be separated at this crucial juncture, who knows what may happen? He's certain to have scores of hopeful young females hanging on his arm in town."

"What of it? If the boy's serious, it won't make a scrap of difference, and if he isn't, it's as well they should both know it."

"Oh, there's no point in talking to you. As if one can afford to let slip the chance of such a brilliant match!" She started to turn impatiently away, but checked suddenly, struck by a happy thought. "Eleanor's been plaguing me lately to let her go and pay Catherine a visit in town," she said thoughtfully. "I did not like the notion, but of course I see now it would be the very thing, for the Pamyngtons are in the same set as the Eversleys. Yes, I shall tell her she may go, after all, and, George, I don't think you need to mention to her that Chalgrove is to accompany his sister. Most likely she won't discover that until she's in London, for she and Phoebe have already taken leave of each other and nothing has been said, I'm sure, or she would have mentioned it. She's such a contrary girl, you know, she might quite likely refuse to go if she thought —"

"That you were matchmaking, eh?" Sir Denham teased her, chucking her playfully under the chin. "Never fear, I'll not betray you, m'dear."

CHAPTER VI

Towards the close of an afternoon some days later, a mud-spattered but otherwise smart travelling carriage pulled up outside one of the elegant, stucco-fronted houses in Hanover Square, and a liveried groom jumped down from the box to assist his passengers to alight.

The first of these was Eleanor Denham, attired in a stylish dark blue pelisse trimmed with fur and a matching bonnet tied with blue ribbons. She looked as fresh as paint, her face alight with eager anticipation. The same could not be said of the second passenger, a solidly built female whose unyielding countenance commanded instant respect from those whom she considered underlings. Indeed, Mrs. Fincher, personal maid to the Denham ladies over a number of years, was a power to be reckoned with in the servants' hall of Eastridge House.

She clicked her tongue in disapproval now at the behaviour of her charge, who, without waiting for the groom to perform this menial office, ran quickly up the steps of the house and pulled at the bell.

A dignified footman in smart livery at once answered the summons.

"Lady Pamyngton expects me," said Eleanor breathlessly.

This became clear the very next moment, for scarcely had the footman had time to admit the arrivals, much less receive their luggage, than a slender female figure came flying down the staircase, and clasped the visitor ecstatically to her bosom.

"Nell, dearest Nell! What an age you've been. I've been looking out for you for hours."

Eleanor Denham returned her sister's embrace in ample measure, knocking her bonnet askew in the process. "Katie, how good it is to see you! We stopped to eat at Reigate, for I was extremely hungry, you know, and that delayed us. And then we were obliged to walk about a little, as poor Fincher felt quite ill with all those hours in a stuffy carriage, and no wonder — it's beyond bearing. I would far rather ride, any day."

"Even one of your iron constitution would hardly attempt a ride of that distance," said Lady Pamyngton, laughing as she disengaged herself and offered her hand to the maid. "How do you feel now, Fincher? If you will go with Harris to the housekeeper's room, I know my Mrs. Allen will make you comfortable. I'm sorry you should have found the journey so trying."

The maid's features relaxed into the nearest expression to cordiality ever achieved by her. She curtseyed and expressed a hope that she found Lady Pamyngton herself in good health, then turned to follow the butler, leaving the two sisters alone.

"Come along," said Catherine Pamyngton, leading Eleanor up the staircase. "And when you've made yourself tidy, we'll have a quiet little chat together. I banished Pamyngton to one of his clubs until dinner, just so that we could be private for a while."

Presently they were sitting together side by side in Catherine's luxurious boudoir, tastefully decorated in soft shades of blue picked out in white. It was a small, intimate room, and Catherine usually sat here during her husband's absences, which were very infrequent. The couple had been married only eighteen months and were still addicted to each other's company, much to the amusement of the more cynical members of the ton.

Seated thus, side by side, the resemblance between the two sisters was marked. Both had the Denham features, a straight little nose, an oval face with creamy complexion and a pair of expressive hazel eyes. The only difference was in hair colouring, Catherine's being of a darker chestnut than Eleanor's, which was brown with strong chestnut tints. There was a difference, too, in expression, for the elder, married sister nowadays bore a more mature look, as might have been expected from one who was a wife and mother.

The two had always been greatly attached to each other, and in the days before Catherine's marriage had been boon companions. In age they were separated by less than two years; Catherine had recently celebrated her twenty-first birthday.

In no time they were chattering away at a great rate, each anxious to hear the other's news.

"How is baby Gerard?" asked Eleanor, sipping the tea which her sister had ordered.

A warm light sprang into Catherine's eyes. "Oh, famous! I don't need to tell you that he is far more advanced than any other baby of his age, besides being the handsomest and most adorable."

Eleanor laughed. "No, you don't need to tell me, Katie. I must say that when I first set eyes on him, I wondered how he would turn out, for I can admit now that I never realised babies looked so red in the face, and so like little old men."

Her sister turned an indignant face towards her. "Little old men, indeed. How dare you, Eleanor Denham!"

"No need to get on your high horse," Eleanor reassured her, with an affectionate pat. "He looked much better at the christening — quite delightful, in fact."

"Well, as his godmother, so you should think. But you may see him for yourself presently, when I take you up to the nursery, and I'm sure you'll eat your words. But tell me about yourself. How have you been passing your time since we all met at Christmas? It seems an age ago."

"Oh, in the usual ways," replied Eleanor, with a shrug. "Going out with the hounds, attending assemblies and neighbourhood parties, flirting a little, coming to blows now and then with Mama and the girls. But now that the hunting's over, it all seemed a trifle flat, so I thought I'd take you up on your invitation to spend a few months in town for a change. I might even get married," she added, as an afterthought.

"Married?" Her sister sounded startled. "Why, have you anyone in mind? You did speak of flirting."

Eleanor laughed again, a light, musical sound that set Katie smiling. "Oh, that — a pastime, surely. No, I've no one in mind as yet, but I dare say someone will soon turn up, for I understand that London's the very best place for that kind of thing. Even though you did manage to bring it off in Brighton!"

"Bring it off!" echoed Katie, scandalised. "Really, Nell, you do make use of the most inelegant expressions!"

"No need to get upset. If we can't speak a little inelegantly to each other in private, it's a poor thing," declared Nell roundly. "You used not to be so — well, I was about to say 'missish', but that won't serve, will it? Seeing that you're a matron now, I mean."

"It's my belief," countered Katie, with a severe look belied by her twinkling eyes, "that you're still too immature to be thinking of marriage."

"Oh, well, I'm nineteen, and if I leave it much longer I'll be practically an old maid, as Mama keeps saying. Besides, I can't think of anything else at all exciting to do at present. At least it would be a novelty, for I'm growing a little jaded by the sameness of everything at home. Mama will be glad to get me out of her way, too, I'm sure."

"Do you and Mama often argue?"

"Not precisely, but you know how it is with Mama. Almost anything I want to do is improper or inconvenient, or something. It's past bearing!"

Katie did know. Mama's letters had become increasingly plaintive of late on the subject of Nell's vagaries. "You must admit, love, that you do get up to some silly tricks at times. But never mind that," she went on quickly, as she saw her sister about to protest. "What kind of gentleman would you like to marry? Or don't you mind?"

Ignoring the jibe implicit in this final question, Eleanor pondered for a moment. "He must be a nobleman, of course," she pronounced at last, with a twinkle in her eye.

"Of course," echoed Katie ironically. "But it would be interesting to hear your reasons."

"Oh, for one thing, your husband is a viscount. I can't allow you to get the better of me, can I?"

"So you believe there should be competition between sisters in the matrimonial stakes? Edifying, to say the least."

"Katie, can you possibly have forgotten how you used to crow over me every time you beat me at croquet in the old days?"

"And have you forgotten how you used to crow over me every time I fell off that pernicious animal, your pony Stella?"

"That's not at all the same thing."

"It is. It's simply a matter of different skills," pointed out Katie. "But there aren't any skills involved in the business of falling in love. That's a question of luck. I chanced to fall in love with a viscount, but Louisa fell in love with a curate. And we're both very happy."

"Who said anything about falling in love?" demanded Nell scornfully.

Her sister stared. "But surely that's what you'd wish?"

"I'm not sure that I do. Look how miserable it made Louisa. She was odiously poor company for months."

"But that was only because Mama opposed the match," objected Katie.

"Yes, and you may be sure that if I were so stupid as to fall in love, it would be with someone whom Mama would consider ineligible, too. No, obviously I must set my sights on an earl — or a duke, perhaps — and then she will say that she always knew I wouldn't disappoint her. Just as she said when you became engaged to Pamyngton."

"Did she indeed?" asked Katie, much diverted. "I never realised that she could be so in charity with me, remembering the many set-downs she used to give me when I was at home."

"Yes, well, perhaps it's no wonder," said Nell, allowing herself to become serious for a moment, "if she did get a trifle flustered with five girls still at home, all to be creditably established. And I must admit that you and I were far more of a handful than the other three put together. Do you remember...?"

They embarked on a spate of reminiscences concerning past scrapes and escapades which soon had them both chuckling delightedly.

"Ah, those were the days!" exclaimed Nell, at last. "But I rely on you, Katie, to present me to some of these eligible gentlemen, so that I can take my pick of them. You go to all the ton parties and to Almack's and so on, so you must be acquainted with scores of them."

"If you mean dukes and earls, I must warn you that most of the noblemen of my acquaintance are already married. There is, of course, Lord Finmere, who is a widower, but," she added, with a quizzing smile, "I fear he might not quite suit your fancy, as he is prodigiously rotund, in spite of wearing a corset like the Prince of Wales. Oh, yes, and Nell, it creaks sometimes when he makes a bow, so that it's almost impossible to keep a straight face. When he was first presented to me, I had to pinch myself hard to prevent a fit of giggles."

Eleanor exploded into laughter. "Can't you think of anyone who is reasonably presentable?" she persisted, once she had recovered from this outburst.

Katie considered. "Most of the names which come to mind are those of younger sons and in the less exalted ranks of the peerage, I fear."

"Pooh, a mere Honourable!" scoffed Nell, with simulated disgust. "I do believe, Katie, you are deliberately trying to fob me off with inferior merchandise so that you can retain your advantage."

"What a shameful conversation this is," pronounced Katie severely. "Were I to take you seriously, Nell, I should be obliged to consider you lost to all proper maidenly feeling."

"Oh, now you sound like Mama. But pray don't start taking me seriously, or whom shall I find to share a jest with when I'm in a jovial mood? My whole dependence is on you, my dear, for you know well that Louisa doesn't quite have our odd sense of humour. Not that I see her so very frequently since she married Oliver Seaton and went off to live in Oxfordshire."

"You still have Jane and Olivia," Katie said.

"True, and we have some rare fun at times, though they can be tiresome, too. Besides, they're still in the schoolroom and must beware of their governess. I do miss you, Katie, truly I do."

"Well, we're to be together again now for two whole months, and I'm sure we'll contrive to enjoy ourselves enormously. I'll take you shopping in Oxford Street and to as many balls and parties as you could wish, for the season is just starting and London will be full of company. I already have vouchers for you at Almack's, and Pamyngton will take you riding in the park — for you know 'tis of no use to expect me to do so. Horses are certainly not my best friends. But I dare say that before long there'll be a long line of gentlemen — perhaps even noblemen — contending for that honour," she concluded, with an appraising look at her sister. "I must say, Nell, you have admirable looks, and should do me credit."

"Thank you, ma'am. And may I say by way of a return compliment, that I don't think any matron has a right to look quite so fetching as you do? Does not Pamyngton consider that it would be more prudent for you to go clad in more sober colours?"

Katie laughed. "We will ask him, and see what he has to say. But enough of your nonsense for now. Come with me to the nursery, and see if little Gerry is not as adorable as I claim."

Later that evening, at a convenient moment when Eleanor was not around, Katie told her husband amusedly that Nell had come up to town to find a husband, since she had nothing of greater interest to do at present.

Viscount Pamyngton, a tall, elegant gentleman with fair hair and very blue eyes, laughed. "She will find herself in a gaggle of other damsels with similar aims," he said. "Every season brings a fresh batch. I fear she'll have cut-throat competition." He pretended to ponder the question seriously for a moment. "What would she say to Freddy Eversley, think you, my love? She's acquainted with him already, and they seemed to get on famously together in Brighton."

"Oh, no!" exclaimed his wife, with a chuckle. "He's only an Honourable, and she's for setting her cap at an earl or a duke, to outdo me."

"Cold-blooded little monster!" he said, in genuine protest.

"Not truly. She's partly joking, and partly too naive to understand fully yet what it is to be in love. Nell's of a very loving disposition, though, and you may be sure she'll never wed without affection, whoever it may be. But hush, she's coming back."

CHAPTER VII

The following few days were taken up with prolonged visits to the fashionable shops which Lady Pamyngton patronised, and a quantity of delectable purchases were made. Eleanor had certainly not come to town with a poorly furnished wardrobe, but it was surprising how many gowns, bonnets, shoes and other items of female attire were necessary to turn her out in prime style, as her sister phrased it. After one particularly tiring excursion, however, wandering in and out of shops all day and trying on this and that, Nell's enjoyment of this pastime became sated for the present, and she declared her desire to go out riding on the following morning.

"Then Pam must escort you," said Katie. "I dare say you can ride any horse in our stable, but I happen to know that he's purchased one especially for your use."

Nell expressed her thanks to her brother-in-law for this service, but the dubious note in her voice made him laugh.

"Never fear, I wouldn't dream of mounting you on a sluggard, Eleanor! You'll find the mare has just sufficient spirit to please you."

She admitted this was true when they rode together the next day, for the mare took exception to a stray dog they encountered as they entered the park. Pamyngton noted with approval her firm handling of the horse, and somewhat relaxed his vigilance.

"She's fresh," said Nell, "that's all. She could do with a good gallop."

"I should perhaps just mention," replied Pamyngton tentatively, "that it's not considered the thing for ladies to gallop their mounts in the park. I know it's poor-spirited of them to submit to this decree, but there it is, you know."

Nell looked disappointed, but to Pamyngton's relief decided not to challenge the edict, contenting herself with cantering the mare. "After all, there's not as much pleasure in having a gallop along a bridle path such as this," she said, indicating the stretch which lay before them, "as in racing across open fields. Besides, there are so many others exercising their horses here, not to mention all these vehicles on the carriageway. What a crowded place Hyde Park is. I dare say you can scarce cover a yard without meeting some acquaintance or other."

"That's true enough, for here come two gentlemen of our acquaintance now."

She looked up with lively interest to see Frederick Eversley approaching on a handsome black horse, accompanied by another rider whom she recognised with considerable surprise.

"Good heavens, Eleanor — Miss Denham!" exclaimed the Earl of Chalgrove, reining in his horse and touching his hat. "This *is* a pleasant meeting. I never expected to see you here."

"No more did I expect to see you," returned Nell. "I thought Lady Chalgrove — but no matter for that," she added hastily, realising that what she had been about to say might embarrass Tom in front of the others. "How do you do, Mr. Eversley?"

Frederick Eversley returned her greeting affably enough, but she could not help noticing the cynical smile with which he had listened to her exchange with Tom. It was as though, she thought indignantly, he did not believe that her surprise at seeing Tom was genuine. Why in the world should he not? she wondered.

There was no time for her to follow up this train of thought, however, for Tom, eager to remain in her company, suggested that they should all four ride together for a while. When the

85

others complied, he ranged himself at Nell's side, leaving Frederick Eversley and Pamyngton to ride behind him.

"The most amazing piece of good fortune, Nell!" he told her enthusiastically. "My cousin asked Mama if I might not come up to town with Phoebe, and she agreed at once. There was not a word about absentee landlords or neglect of duties. I still can't understand it. Of course, he's a fellow of considerable standing, I admit, but my mother's not in general persuadable, as you must know, when she has a notion firmly fixed in her head. So here I am, and likely to stay for a month or so, at any rate. I dare say we will see a good deal of each other. You're staying with your sister, Lady Pamyngton, I imagine. I expect Lady Eversley will bring Phoebe to call on you before long."

This prophecy was fulfilled on the very next morning, when Lady Eversley presented herself in Hanover Square, accompanied by her niece and nephew. Catherine and Eleanor were just making up their minds as to how they should employ the remainder of the morning, for the earlier part had been spent in studying the invitation cards which had arrived at the house recently, and deciding which should be accepted.

"*Not* Mrs. Quiller's evening party," Katie had declared decidedly. "They're always odiously boring, and the refreshments are poorer than at Almack's, which is saying something!"

"But I thought the assemblies at Almack's were all the fashion," protested Nell. "You said yourself 'tis always difficult to get vouchers, but that every female doing the season must be seen there."

"Quite true, my love, but one doesn't go to Almack's to eat, but to dance with some of these eligible gentlemen whom you profess yourself eager to meet. You'll soon see, for we shall be going there on Tuesday evening. I say, Nell!" Katie continued, turning over another card. "This sounds more in our style — a private masquerade at Lady Thorncliff's. I must persuade Pam to escort us to that, what do you say?"

It was when this had been decided upon, and plans for the rest of the morning debated, that their callers were announced.

Phoebe expressed the same surprise at Eleanor's coming to town as her brother had shown yesterday. "You made no mention of it when we parted," she said, a little hurt.

"No, for it was settled quite suddenly. But now that I am here, I mean to make the most of it, I can tell you. Katie and I have been round the shops and purchased no end of things — a most delightful bonnet, Phoebe, in chip straw with a turned-back brim lined with pink ruched ribbon — but you shall see it, I promise you, before long. Not to mention a divine ball gown in sprigged muslin. You must spend an afternoon here with me, and we will gloat over them all together. That is, if Lady Eversley permits," she added as an afterthought, with an apologetic glance at Phoebe's aunt.

"Oh, but of course," answered Lady Eversley promptly. "I shall be only too pleased for Phoebe to have the companionship of a young lady with whom she's already intimate, as it can sometimes be lonely for a newcomer to London until she strikes up some fresh acquaintance. 'Tis easier when there are other girls in the same household, but of course my own daughters are married."

"It occurs to me, ma'am," put in Katie, "that you might be glad to be relieved occasionally of the necessity of chaperoning your niece to some of the social events of the season. If so, I'd be delighted to take charge of her along with my sister, whenever it chances that they are to attend the same parties and balls."

Lady Eversley looked gratified. "You are most good, Lady Pamyngton. Of course, Phoebe will have her brother to escort her most of the time, but the presence of a matron — though you're a very young matron, my dear — is always desirable. And I confess that nowadays I've somewhat lost my taste for too hectic an existence. My increasing years, you know."

This being settled, Tom, who had so far been chatting with Pamyngton, broke in upon his sister's tête-à-tête with Eleanor in a determined fashion, more or less monopolising the latter for the duration of the visit. Before they left, he had extracted a promise from her to drive out in the park with him on the following morning, should the weather prove fine. His attentions to her did not go unnoticed by Catherine Pamyngton, and when she and Nell were once more alone, she began to quiz her sister about him.

"Well, you are a sly puss, Nell! All this talk of coming to town to look for a nobleman, and you already had one on your own doorstep at home. I must say that it came as a surprise to me that Chalgrove was keen on you, for there was no sign of it when last we visited Mama and Papa. Indeed, I never thought of him in that way at all, for we've known the Chalgroves since childhood, and in such cases people are rarely attracted to each other. But now I think of it, Mama has thrown out one or two hints lately in her letters, although I paid small heed to that, for Mama always has been addicted to matchmaking for one or other of us, usually with small justification."

"Yes, indeed. I wish she would not do it so much," replied Nell indignantly. "If you must know, Katie, she has been thrusting Tom at me these past three months, ever since he showed any inclination for my company."

"It seems a pretty strong inclination," said Katie, looking keenly at her. "And you — what are your feelings towards him?"

Nell shrugged. "Oh, I don't know. As you say, we were childhood playmates, and I've always considered him more in the light of a brother. Besides, he is so young! I don't mean in years, precisely, because he's three and twenty, but his upbringing has been so hedged about by his mother, so sheltered, that he appears younger than his age. His cousin, for instance, Mr. Eversley, is only three years his senior, but in comparison he is a man of the world."

"You like Mr. Eversley?" asked Katie, with quickened interest. "Is there anything —"

"No, there is not!" snapped Nell. "In fact, I am particularly out of charity with that gentleman at present. No, never mind why," she added as she saw the question forming on her sister's lips. "It's of no consequence, just a tiff we had when he was staying with the Chalgroves recently. I think him insufferably high-handed!"

"Do you?" Katie seemed surprised. "He is a general favourite in town, considered to be easy-going and tolerant, and with a strong sense of humour. You must have struck upon a side of his nature which is not usually revealed — or else you were in one of your contrary moods," she added, with sisterly candour.

"Perhaps I may have been, but no matter for that. It was simply that his was the first name that came to mind to explain to you what I meant about Tom."

"Yes, I do see what you mean. Of course, a man like Frederick Eversley, who has been on the town for a number of years, will naturally appear more interesting to a female than one like Tom who, in spite of having a title and large estate, has spent his entire life in rural surroundings. But all the same, my dear Nell, the affair will soon right itself when Tom acquires some polish, as he is sure to do away from Chalgrove Park, and under his cousin's guidance. And perhaps you should remember his material assets, since you're so set on outdoing me in the matter of husbands," she added teasingly.

"You know well I was only joking, Katie. Pray, don't sound like Mama. There's another objection to Tom, too. He may be pursuing *me* at present, but he has a decidedly roving eye, and it may easily be on someone else next week, or month. How can I possibly contemplate marriage to a man like that? I would rather be an old maid all my life."

Katie laughed. "I don't fear any such prospect as that! Shall we partake of some luncheon, and then drive out for a while this afternoon?"

CHAPTER VIII

Hopeful mamas launching their daughters in polite society that season had been extremely gratified to learn of the presence in town of that very rare target for their ambitions: an unattached young nobleman in possession of an unencumbered estate. Invitations for the earl and his sister began to pour in daily, and Tom was nothing loth to accept all of them. In consequence, he soon became a familiar and much courted figure at balls, routs, soirees and other entertainments.

Greatly to their chagrin, however, the chaperons could not help observing that whenever Miss Eleanor Denham chanced to be present, their own young charges received scant attention from this highly eligible parti. In spite of the lady's light-hearted dalliance with others of her admirers, of whom there were several, word soon went round that it looked as if Miss Denham and the earl would make a match of it.

The gossip reached Freddy Eversley's ear and he smiled cynically, reflecting that the lady had played her cards well, but that she might have difficulties when it came to the sticking point. Tom had yet to get round Lady Chalgrove — no light undertaking. He himself had so far steered clear of Eleanor Denham, although he had naturally been present at many of the same social engagements. On the evening of Lady Thorncliff's masquerade, however, they were once more brought together.

Unkind people judged Lady Thorncliff's periodic masquerades to be little better than romps, but this was too harsh. She certainly insisted upon anonymity being preserved as far as possible until the general unmasking before supper.

To aid this, the ballroom was dimly lit with coloured lanterns, no names were announced and neither were introductions made. Sets for the dances were formed arbitrarily by two Masters of Ceremonies, who selected as partners ladies and gentlemen who had not arrived together. Many of the guests were wearing historic costume, which made recognition more difficult, but even those in masks and dominoes were not readily identifiable in the subdued lighting of the room. Nevertheless, though in such an atmosphere of mystery laughter and fun naturally prevailed, seldom did anyone's conduct stray too far from the line of propriety.

Tom and Phoebe were not present on this occasion, owing to a clash of engagements. Tom would have much preferred to attend the masquerade, which he was sure would be capital fun, but Phoebe had preferred the quiet soiree to which an old friend of Lady Eversley's had previously invited them, and so he gave way. Eleanor had come, attended by her sister and Pamyngton. As she looked about the room, her eyes sparkled with anticipation.

"This is more in my style than Almack's, Katie. I dare say there'll be no end of gaiety."

"Indeed there will," agreed Pamyngton, gazing curiously at the motley assembly. "I rather think I have identified that fellow in cavalier costume, but who is the milkmaid beside him to whom he's paying so much attention? Not, I fancy, his wife."

"Oh, yes, I see," replied Katie, peering in the direction of his gaze. "Of course, 'tis Brynton, is it not? But certainly Lady Brynton is of quite a different figure — she has more of everything, if you know what I mean! I dare say 'tis one of his flirts, for he has a shocking reputation. Beware of him, Nell, if you should chance to get him as a partner. You realise we must dance with partners chosen for us by the Masters of Ceremonies?"

"Don't worry," laughed Eleanor, "I can take care of myself."

She had barely uttered the words when she was whisked away by one of the Masters, and her hand presented to a tall, slim gentleman wearing a blue domino. She looked curiously up at his face, caught the glitter of his eyes behind the concealing mask, and failed to recognise him as anyone she knew, so she looked modestly down again as she allowed him to lead her into the set.

For his part, he felt very well satisfied with his partner, though he, too, failed at first to recognise her. Her gold silk domino flowed around what was an extremely pleasing figure; the lace-edged black mask gave a touch of mystery to her oval face, and the silky hair — what colour was it? Difficult to tell in this light — clustered in soft tendrils around her forehead. Altogether a young lady whose acquaintance would be well worth cultivating, once her identity was revealed.

This occurred speedily, for no sooner had the partners exchanged a few words than each knew the other without any doubt.

"This is an unexpected honour, Miss Denham," said Freddy Eversley smoothly.

"Yes, isn't it?" returned Nell, laughing up at him. "We haven't danced together since I arrived in town, and now it is only because we've been thrust at each other."

"Do you dislike that?"

She tossed her head so that her curls glistened in the soft light. "Oh, no, it is all part of the fun! Not to know who one's partner may be, I mean. All the same —" she glanced up at him challengingly — "it has sometimes occurred to me that you were deliberately avoiding me when we've attended the same assemblies."

"Has it?"

"Oh, pray don't be so cryptic. I know that you were vexed with me over the way I spoke of you at your aunt's that evening."

"You are mistaken," he said coolly. "I was amused, merely."

"You may say so, but I don't think it's true," she burst out candidly. "And after all, I did apologise to you at the Lydhursts' party, and I explained how it was, so I think you might forgive me."

"Oh, but I have — forgiven and forgotten."

"Then may we not be friends? We seemed to deal so well together when we were younger."

She looked at him with such a winning expression in her eyes that for a moment his heart gave a sudden leap. Had she been any other female than his cousin's prospective affianced, he thought, he would certainly have been tempted to flirt with her.

"But of course," he replied, smiling down at her. "And since there seems a likelihood that we may one day be more closely connected, it's an excellent notion."

She gave a quick frown. "More closely connected? What do you mean, sir?"

"Oh, come," he said, a shade cynically, "there's no need to dissemble, surely?"

"Dissemble?" She appeared genuinely puzzled.

He searched her face, but the concealing mask made it difficult to interpret her expression. "I can only suppose you to be unduly modest," he said, somewhat more harshly than he intended. "It's the talk of the town that you and my cousin Tom are about to become engaged."

"Oh, is it?" she asked indignantly. "And we've scarce been here above a fortnight. What odious gossips people are, to be sure!"

"Well, yes, they are," he admitted readily. "Gossip is the lifeblood of the ton. But do you really object to the rumour?"

"Of course I do!" Even in that light, it was easy to see the flushed face and indignant eyes. "I will not be disposed of in that casual way. Tom is a very good friend, that is all, and we have known each other forever. But that is not to say that we have any thought of marriage."

He remembered that he had thought once before how very attractive she looked in anger. He felt again the quick leap of his pulses, and warned himself to be on his guard against her charm. "Have you not?" It was said coolly enough, but then he added, more impulsively, "I quite believed otherwise, judging from what Tom once said to me, and also from your own behaviour towards him."

"Are you suggesting, sir, that my behaviour towards your cousin has been in any way at fault?" she demanded, in a dangerous tone.

"Not at all. I would say that it has been nicely calculated to produce the desired effect."

The movements of the dance separated them for a few moments at this point. During this interval he had time to regret his impulsiveness, and Eleanor to ponder over his meaning with a suspicion that it was other than flattering.

When they came together again, she returned at once to the attack. "I do not at all understand your meaning," she said brusquely. "Pray be more explicit."

But he was more on his guard now. "Oh, no, I think not," he answered casually. "It's of no importance. Tell me instead what you think of your first masquerade."

"I will not be fobbed off so easily, Mr. Eversley. I insist upon knowing what lay behind your remark."

Her expressive eyes flashed as she darted a challenging look at him, and again his senses stirred in response. She really was a bewitching female, he thought, and all the more dangerous on that account. Perhaps it was as well that Tom had already laid claim to her, or even a hardened bachelor like himself might for once be tempted to fall into something more serious than a light flirtation. Should he give her a truthful answer to her question? It might be the best way of putting an end to what was fast becoming a hazardous situation. He made a decision. "I think you do know," he said, in an even tone which did not reflect his underlying feelings. "You admitted to me at Lydhurst's ball that you were obliged to do something to help matters along, and that was why you'd exaggerated our past association out of all proportion."

She frowned. "Yes, but I don't see how that concerns my behaviour towards Tom."

"Oh, come, ma'am, you're not being honest," he protested, in an impulsive burst of candour. "Wasn't it my cousin with whom you wished to help matters along? Didn't you try to represent me as a rival for your affections in order to bring him up to scratch? Deuce take it, you did admit the whole thing to me, you know, when you apologised for having to blacken my character that evening."

Even in the dim light, he could see that the flush had died away from her face, leaving it pale. "Is that what you think of me?" she whispered, in a strained voice. "Do you believe I am ruthlessly seeking to entrap your cousin into marriage?"

"Wouldn't be so surprising," he said brutally. "Most females would be tempted at the prospect of becoming a countess, and it wouldn't take much to tip the scales, seeing that Tom's attracted to you already."

"Oh, you are odious!" she exclaimed contemptuously. "If only you knew how far off the mark you are, Mr. Eversley. I thought we might be friends, but with such an opinion of me, there's no possibility of that."

The dance was ending and she snatched her hand from his, giving him a mocking curtsey.

"If I'm in error —" he began doubtfully, as he returned the customary bow. But she flung away from him to join her sister.

This episode quite ruined the masquerade for Nell. She danced with several different partners, chatting away to them in her usual light-hearted style, but the zest had gone out of the evening. After the unmasking, she went in to supper with Katie and Pamyngton, escorted by one of her admirers, the Honourable Philip Summers. Mr. Summers was a tall, dark gentleman with laughing blue eyes and that air of assurance which marked most male members of the ton. Eleanor had met him frequently since coming to London, and always enjoyed his company. At present, however, he found her somewhat unresponsive.

"Shall I offer you a penny, Miss Denham?" he quizzed her, at last.

She started. "Oh, you mean for my thoughts? I assure you they're not worth it, sir."

He gave her a keen look. "No, I rather believe that. Gloomy, I should say. Have you just discovered that some other lady in the room is wearing an exact replica of your gown? That, of course, must make any female feel annoyed."

She laughed. "Indeed it would. But no such tragedy has occurred — at least, as far as I can tell, for I've not put everyone's dress under scrutiny."

He raised an eyebrow. "No? I thought it to be a compelling occupation of all ladies. Well, if not that, then what has brought a cloud to that fair countenance? Nothing, I trust, that can be laid at my door?"

She reassured him on this point, and took more care to put aside her fit of abstraction and enter fully into the spirit of the evening. She was soon gaily chattering away to Mr. Summers, and in this more promising atmosphere he ventured to suggest that she might like to ride with him in the park on the following morning, provided the weather proved suitable. She acceded to his request, and Katie gave her a meaning look.

"Be careful that you don't lose your earl!" she teased, on their way home in the carriage.

She was rather surprised at the irritable response to this quip, and wisely kept quiet afterwards, thinking that her sister must be fatigued.

This suited Nell perfectly, for all she wanted at present was the leisure to ponder over her disturbing conversation with Mr. Eversley. She soon excused herself when they reached home, and sat down in the privacy of her bedchamber to give her thoughts rein.

It had been a severe shock to learn how greatly he had misunderstood the motives for her conduct on that fateful evening at Chalgrove Park. She realised now that the imperfect explanation she had attempted to give him at the Lydhursts' party was capable of being misinterpreted. He had appeared at the time to understand what she wished to say, yet his replies had been more cynical than she had expected.

She thought angrily how foolish she had been not to put the matter more plainly to him. Yet how could she have done so, without betraying Phoebe's confidence? She recalled doubting at the time whether he could be aware of his aunt's matchmaking plans, but nothing in his conduct had ever suggested it. And if he were not, how on earth could she have supposed that her well-meant intervention would be understood? She had taken too much for granted, and been very foolish.

The remarks he had made to her at the Lydhursts' party now became comprehensible, for he had believed her to be confessing to a scheme to encourage Tom to declare himself. The mere thought made her feel as if she were blushing from head to foot. Surely even the little he knew of her, thought Nell indignantly, should have told him that she was not a calculating female!

And now he would never learn that her little ploy had been intended to benefit Phoebe, not herself. She could not enlighten him, and Phoebe was unlikely to do so, for the cousins were not on such terms of intimacy. He would go on believing that Eleanor Denham meant to become a countess at all costs.

It was a melancholy reflection — so melancholy that she felt the tears starting. She brushed them angrily away. What did she care for Frederick Eversley's opinion?

She was startled to find that indeed she did care, more than seemed possible judging by the degree of their acquaintance. But, of course, she told herself, it was only hurt pride.

CHAPTER IX

Phoebe and Tom came to call the following morning, and Tom let it be seen that he was more than a little disgruntled to learn that Eleanor had arranged to go riding with Philip Summers.

"Dashed unfortunate," he said, in a chagrined tone. "I was about to ask you myself, as it has turned out a fine morning."

"Another time, perhaps," she replied carelessly. "After all, 'tis no great matter, for we often ride together at home, do we not?"

"It matters to me," he said in a low voice, with a meaning look.

Nell ignored this, and went on to ask Phoebe how she had enjoyed the soiree of the previous evening. All three females then chatted animatedly together, leaving Tom — in a decided huff — to devote his conversation to Pamyngton. Presently a footman appeared to say that Mr. Summers had arrived for Miss Denham. Nell rose and excused herself, avoiding Tom's angry glare, saying blithely that they would all be meeting again that evening, in any case.

They were to attend a private ball given by one of the London hostesses, and for the first time Catherine Pamyngton would have Phoebe in her care. The charge was not altogether a light one, as Katie well realised. A girl as beautiful as Phoebe naturally attracted scores of young gentlemen to her side, but added to her physical allure was the material one of being both an earl's daughter and an heiress. Katie relied upon her husband to keep the fortune hunters away, and could only hope that the girl herself would be discreet with the rest of her entourage.

She soon saw that she need not have concerned herself. Phoebe, though never lacking in amiability and politeness towards her admirers, remained cool and reserved, showing no preferences.

"'Tis almost as if," she remarked to Nell, after having kept an eye on Phoebe for half the evening, "the child lacks heart! I'm sure at her age I could never have resisted young Lord Daylesford, so handsome as he is, and perfectly eligible, too. But just look at her, going into the set with him with such a prim countenance, as though she didn't even know he existed!"

"And neither does he for Phoebe. She has —" Nell hesitated — "well, I suppose I may confide her secret to you, for I know you'd never repeat it. The thing is, there's someone at home in Sussex."

Katie's eyes widened. "You mean she's already affianced?"

"No, no. When I said *secret*, I meant no less. Her mother would never consent, so the gentleman in question cannot fix his interest with Phoebe. She never wished to come to town, Katie, but Lady Chalgrove forced her into it. And that's not the worst — her mother is intent on her marrying her cousin, Mr. Eversley."

"Freddy Eversley?" echoed Katie, amazed.

"Hush!" admonished Nell. "Someone may hear you."

"But Freddy!" protested Katie, in a much lower tone. "That's too absurd. Why, everyone knows he's a confirmed bachelor — it's one of his constant boasts to his cronies."

"So I believe," said Nell drily.

"Do you really mean to say that he is contemplating matrimony at last?"

Nell shook her head. "No. Phoebe assures me that he's completely indifferent to her, and anyone seeing them together must realise that is true."

"Yes," agreed Katie thoughtfully. "He rarely troubles to ask her to dance, and when he does, now I think of it, there's nothing in the least lover-like in his manner. Is he aware of his aunt's wishes?"

"I don't believe he is. I did think so, once, but I see now I was mistaken."

"Then how can Lady Chalgrove possibly hope to bring it off? Plenty of arranged marriages are made, but the prospective bridegroom must be privy to the arrangement, surely. Indeed, 'tis more usual in such cases for the gentleman to be the instigator, I believe. She must be muddled in her head! I always did think she was an odd woman."

"So she is, but she knows just how to keep her own family under her thumb," said Nell vehemently. "She hoped that by sending Phoebe to London in Lady Eversley's care, she would be bringing the two cousins together and so achieve the result she desired. I tried to disrupt things, to assist my poor friend, but I doubt it has done much good," she concluded dolefully.

Katie evinced the liveliest interest in this, and would not rest until her sister had related the whole. She listened with appreciative chuckles, and at the end, laughed heartily.

"What a girl you are, Nell!" she exclaimed admiringly. "I'd have given almost anything to hear you on that occasion."

"Well, I did think it great fun at the time," admitted Nell. "But I'm not at all sure that it served the purpose — besides, it put me into a bit of a scrape."

"You're always in a scrape, my dear, so that shouldn't worry you. But what kind of scrape? With Lady Chalgrove, I suppose," Katie went on, after receiving no immediate answer from her sister. "She would hardly consider you to be a fitting wife for her son after hearing of your amorous adventures with her nephew." She went off into another peal of laughter, but stopped suddenly on seeing her sister's glum face. She took Nell's hand, pressing it affectionately. "Have I been clumsy?" she asked contritely. "Do you truly care for Chalgrove, and now you have antagonised his mother? Is that it?"

Nell pulled her hand away abruptly. "No, Tom means nothing to me, except as a childhood friend. I thought I had already made that plain to you."

"Yes, you did, but there seemed to be a doubt in your mind, and there's no denying the fact that he's head over heels in love with you," stated Katie. "But if you don't wish to wed him, and therefore are not concerned over what Lady Chalgrove may think of you, what *is* your scrape, my love? Surely you may tell me."

Possibly Nell might have attempted to do so, but at that moment their respective partners, who had been waiting patiently to one side during the sisters' tête-à-tête, arrived to lead them into the set before it should be too late. During the remainder of the evening, there was no opportunity for them to resume their conversation, and for the moment it was erased from Katie's mind.

Tom had already tried on several occasions to secure Nell for a partner, but without success. When at last he did manage to arrive first at her side, and for once she lacked the excuse of a previous promise, he led her on to the floor with an almost aggressive air.

"Anyone would think you don't wish to dance with me," he accused her. "I haven't been able to come near you all evening."

She did not reply immediately, seeming to be concentrating on her steps. "Don't you find it more fun to dance with new partners?" she replied presently. "We may dance together any time at home."

"That's what you said about riding with me." His tone was sulky. "You may prefer new friends, but I have no desire to be with any other female than you, Nell."

She felt a moment's panic. The prospect of a declaration in the middle of a crowded ballroom held no appeal for her, and it looked very much as though matters were veering in that direction. She gazed frantically about her, and encountered Frederick Eversley's cynical eye. He was in the same set, partnering a young lady with dark ringlets and an enchanting smile, but for the moment his attention was upon his neighbours.

For some reason, his amused glance raised her hackles, and she answered Tom with a touch of asperity. "Doubtless that's because you know me better. After all, we've been acquainted since childhood — we're almost like brother and sister."

"But I don't regard you in that light!"

"No? Well, as you have one sister already, you may not be anxious to acquire a second. But I've no brothers, Tom, and have always considered you as a substitute."

"Thank you," he answered with heavy sarcasm. "I suppose now I know where I stand."

"Almost on my foot!" she exclaimed, laughing up at him. "Pray mind your steps, Tom, for your weight is not inconsiderable, you know."

He apologised sheepishly, then fell into a moody silence for the duration of the dance. It was a new experience for the young earl to find a female rejecting him. Usually, he had been the one to drift away from those young ladies whom he had briefly deigned to honour with his attentions. His devotion to Eleanor Denham had lasted a full three months, and he had begun to believe himself serious. His mother's disapproval, so efficacious in putting an end to his previous fancies, had not succeeded in this instance.

But no female should be allowed to make a fool of him, he thought resentfully. Evidently Eleanor intended to keep him at bay while she was here in town, having her fling and flirting with every available man, then to return home to Sussex and pick him up again like a discarded toy. Not if he knew it! Now that his eyes were fully opened to her character, he found it possible to gaze on her physical attractions without a tremor. There were other young ladies in the room as pretty as she — he had noticed several in passing, even while he had been taken up with Eleanor — and he had no doubt at all that they would be only too willing to make themselves agreeable to one who could not help knowing himself to be an eligible gentleman. His cousin Freddy was right. It was a mistake to think too soon of marriage, when one might enjoy the company of countless attractive girls in the meantime. Freedom, that was the thing. And here he could fully enjoy it, for there was no maternal censor at hand.

Having reached this momentous decision, he proceeded to put it into practice, and Nell was amused to observe, in the intervals of chatting with her various partners, how quickly Tom had consoled himself for her supposed defection.

One gentleman of her acquaintance who did not seek her out as a partner that evening was Mr. Eversley. There had been one occasion, just after supper, when he had hovered near her, and she had been guilty of falsely informing an applicant that she was already promised, in the hope that Frederick might be about to ask her. Instead, he had requested the honour from Katie. Nell was not left partnerless for more than a few seconds afterwards, but her chagrin was as great as though she had sat out the whole dance.

CHAPTER X

What had begun with Tom in a fit of pique, soon developed into a pleasurable habit, and he flitted from one flirtation to another with an ease and rapidity which raised first hope and later disappointment in many an anxious mama's bosom. Little more than a fortnight went by before word was circulating that the match between the Earl of Chalgrove and Miss Denham seemed no longer at all likely.

"And for my part, I never did think it," declared Lady Summers to one of her gossip-mongering cronies. "It was easy to see that on Miss Denham's side no particular attraction existed. Of course, one could not have blamed any girl for trying to fix the interest of an earl, but it's my belief that her natural preference is for a somewhat older, more mature gentleman."

"Such as your son?" murmured the other. "They are seen about together a good deal, I hear. What is your opinion of the girl?"

"Oh, she's a charming enough creature, well connected and with a respectable fortune," replied Lady Summers, with a careless air which covered the pains she had taken to satisfy herself on these points. "But she's certainly not the first young lady to interest Philip, and I dare say she won't be the last. I fear he's a shocking flirt, like most young men about town. I'm always telling him 'tis high time he married and settled down, but I don't need to tell you how little the advice of a parent is ever heeded."

As it was common knowledge that this particular lady was blessed with a wayward son who had a passion for gaming, this was scarcely a kind remark. Lady Summers, however, was not noted for the kindness of her disposition.

Gaming was, in fact, another diversion in which Tom was dabbling since he had ceased to dance attendance on Eleanor. He had been introduced into the fashionable London clubs by his uncle as a matter of course, and had soon struck up acquaintance with a number of young men. One or two of these frequented less reputable establishments, popularly dubbed gaming hells, where inexperienced clients were welcomed as pigeons for the plucking. Eager for every fresh experience of town life, Tom agreed to accompany his new acquaintances to these haunts.

Word of this reached his aunt's ear, and she became sufficiently alarmed to mention it to her husband. Lord Eversley pointed out that he had no intention of acting as a guardian to his nephew. After issuing such warnings as he deemed necessary, he had in the past turned his own three sons loose on the town to learn by their mistakes, and it had answered very well. He could see no reason for varying the treatment in Tom's case. However, in response to Lady Eversley's importunities, he reluctantly agreed at last to consult Freddy on the subject.

"No reason to think he's losing a lot of money, is there?" asked Freddy.

"Not so far as I know, but your mother's anxious. She feels accountable to her sister, you see."

Freddy sighed. "Well, he can afford to lose some of his wealth, can't he? He's not exactly penniless. Write it all down to experience. Still, I'll keep an eye open, if you like."

His father looked relieved. "Trouble is, the boy's been smothered all his life. 'Tis not surprising he wants to shake a loose leg for a while. He was no trouble at first — too busy hanging on little Miss Denham's sleeve to take much interest in anything else. But that seems to have passed off lately."

"Indeed? Come to think of it, I did hear some gossip to that effect," said Freddy carelessly. "At first, everyone was predicting a match in that quarter."

"There are plenty of tattlers in town, my boy. Never bother to listen, myself. Gossip's all very well for females, they love it. All the same, I fancy your mother thought they would hit it off. Nice little chit, the Denham girl — too good for Tom, in a way. Not that there's anything wrong with the boy that time won't cure, but she's altogether too decided a character for him. It never does for the wife to have a stronger personality than the husband."

Freddy laughed. "The voice of experience, sir?"

"Not my own, you impudent boy. Your mother and I were well matched from the start. She knows her own mind, but then so do I. Compromise, my boy, that's the ticket in matrimony."

Freddy nodded, suitably impressed by his parent's rare venture into philosophy.

He did put himself to the exertion of strolling into one of the plusher gaming houses on an evening when he knew that Tom would be there with a few friends. He found his cousin seated with several others, a few of whom were known to him, at a table where a game of dice was in progress.

Tom greeted him cordially, inviting him to join the game. Freddy consulted his watch.

"Only an hour to spare, as I've another engagement," he replied. "Still, if no one has any objection?"

None being voiced, he sat down, and the play continued. At the end of the hour, he rose to go.

"I'll come with you," said Tom impulsively. "I want a word with you."

There were a few half-hearted protests at this, but Tom was adamant, and the two cousins left together.

"Came to keep an eye on me, didn't you?" Tom accused his cousin, in an aggrieved tone. "Don't trouble to deny it."

"Then I won't," replied Freddy calmly. "You needn't suppose it was entirely my own notion."

"I suppose 'tis my mother again," said Tom, nettled. "She's been badgering my aunt to see that I don't get into bad company, and game away the estate, or some such nonsense. Well, I'm not exactly an idiot. I know well that there are sharpsters to be met with in those gaming hells, and although I enjoy a flutter now and then, I'm not such a fool as to develop an obsession and lose all my money. I don't need a nursemaid, Freddy!"

"Never thought you did, old fellow," said Freddy soothingly. "And I don't mind telling you, 'tis not a part I exactly relish for myself, but I promised to see how you were going on, you know."

"Yes, we're both caught in the same family coil, that's the awful thing," Tom said bitterly. "I tell you what, Freddy, I've had too much petticoat government in the past, and it has got to end."

"That's the idea," remarked his cousin, looking at him speculatively. "What do you say to coming back to my rooms and sharing a bottle?"

"I thought you had an engagement?"

Freddy shrugged. "One of those expediencies, my dear chap. Dicing isn't my game. I prefer cards, where at least there's an element of skill."

"Yes, you're right, by Jove. Very well, I'll be glad to go back with you."

Once admitted by a competent manservant to Freddy's apartments, Tom was soon sitting at his ease in a comfortable room with a decidedly masculine flavour.

"You're fine and snug here," he remarked, looking appreciatively about him. "Lucky chap! What wouldn't I give to have a place of my own in town like this."

"I can't think of any reason why you shouldn't, my dear fellow. Got a man of business here, haven't you? Get him to find you something."

"That's all very well," objected his cousin, "but you know my mother —" He broke off, and smote the palm of his hand with a clenched fist. "It is time to put a stop to all this foolishness! As if I can't take a bolt to London now and then, without neglecting Chalgrove Park! Why, other men keep asking me if I've a house or a set of chambers here, and seem astounded to think that I haven't. Makes a chap feel a bit of a dullard, you know. My mother must be made to see sense! Come to think of it," he added, as a thought struck him, "maybe she's beginning to, as lately she hasn't written me any of those devilish letters urging my return which I seemed to get every few days at first. Perhaps she's getting used to my absence."

Freddy nodded, and poured the wine which had been left by the manservant. He handed a glass to Tom, who sipped it thoughtfully.

"Tell you what," Tom said, after another moment's reflection during which his cousin relaxed in an armchair, stretching out his long legs before him, "I'll see our lawyer, Grimmond, tomorrow, and set him on to the business. No use continuing to feel I must first consult Mama over everything.

I've got to get over that. She must, too. Time to assert myself. I'm three and twenty, not a callow youth in my teens!"

"That's the ticket," approved Freddy, trying not to smile at this long overdue surge of rebellion.

"Don't think I'm not fond of Mama," continued Tom, warming to his theme as he emptied his wine glass and held it out for a refill. "There's no one like her — she's given up her life to Phoebe and me. But the thing is, 'tis time we looked out for ourselves. Well, time I did, anyway," he amended. "Females are another matter. Though mind you, Nell Denham's right about one thing — *I* am Phoebe's guardian, not Mama, and I'm the one to give my consent to her marriage."

Freddy sat up abruptly. "What's this — Miss Denham, Phoebe's marriage —? I know you'd had a few glasses before you came here, but you aren't foxed, surely, Tom?"

His cousin laughed. "No, not at all, I promise you. But you don't know about Phoebe, of course. She wants to marry Lydhurst."

"Very good sort of fellow," approved Freddy.

"So I think, but my mother has other plans for her. That's why she sent her to town. Phoebe's unhappy over it."

"I take it my aunt wants a more brilliant match for your sister?"

"That's it. I don't know —" Tom looked puzzled — "but I fancy Phoebe's keeping something dark. I've a notion she knows who it is my mother's got in mind for her. Though since Mama has small acquaintance in Town —" He broke off. "Unless she's cooked up something with my aunt — your mother, that's to say."

Freddy frowned, suddenly struck by a fleeting recollection from his first interview with his mother over their visit to Chalgrove Park. There had been a certain reticence in her

112

manner when Phoebe's matrimonial prospects were under discussion. He puzzled for a moment or two, but could make nothing of it, so abandoned the thought.

"And where does Miss Denham come into this?" he asked curiously.

"Oh, she and Phoebe are bosom pals, you know, and of course Phoebe confided everything to her. And Nell said I was Phoebe's legal guardian, and could give my permission for Lydhurst to wed her, if I chose."

"Hm. A bright female, Miss Denham. You can, of course. Do you intend to do so?"

Tom hesitated. "I'm not sure. 'Tis one thing to decide for myself about having a place of my own here, but when it comes to my sister's future — well, a mother is usually considered the best judge of a daughter's welfare."

Freddy shook his head mournfully at his cousin. "Never say you're unwilling to strike a blow for poor little Phoebe, now that you're determined to make your own declaration of independence. Or do you think Lydhurst's a passing fancy on her part?"

"No, I don't. It struck me they were both head over heels in love, when I talked to the pair of them. And Phoebe isn't a flirtatious kind of girl, either — you must have noticed that for yourself."

"Unlike her brother," grinned Freddy. "Yes, I had noticed."

Tom shrugged. "Well, I came here to enjoy myself, and with so many pretty girls abounding, what's a fellow to do? You're a good one to talk, I must say."

"*Touché*. But just a minute — I thought you told me that you wished to fix your interest on Miss Denham?"

"So I thought, at one time," said Tom with a scowl. "But she's made it plain enough that she doesn't want me — talked about our being like brother and sister, if you please! I'm not the man to hanker after a female who shows no interest in me, especially when there are plenty of others. Besides, I'm coming round to your way of thinking, now. Time enough for marriage when the delights of bachelor freedom begin to pall, and I'm only just beginning to sample them."

"So Miss Denham gave you the cold shoulder, did she? And I thought she'd set her sights on being a countess," said Freddy ruminatively.

"Nell Denham? Not she! You can't have much notion of her character, if you think that," replied Tom scornfully. "Lady Denham, now, that's another matter. She's like all these matchmaking mamas. But Nell isn't on the catch for a title, you can take my word for that. After all, I've known her all my life."

"True. I must bow to your superior knowledge. Evidently I misjudged her. But to return to your sister — what are you going to do about her?"

Tom made an impatient movement. "Oh, that can wait for a while, at least until we return home. She must be enjoying all these balls and parties. No female could do otherwise. Time enough to decide."

Freddy nodded absently. His thoughts had moved away from his cousin Phoebe's concerns to a more interesting private matter.

Her brother might consider that no female could fail to enjoy the delights of a London season, but Phoebe knew otherwise. It was not perhaps apparent in her behaviour, for she was normally quiet and a little withdrawn, showing only a mild enthusiasm for events which would have sent a more volatile young girl into positive raptures. Once or twice Lady Eversley had felt vaguely uneasy over her niece's quiet acceptance of the entertainment offered her, but when she ventured to mention this to Tom, he had brushed it aside with an assurance that Phoebe was not a girl to go into whoops of delight.

"Depend upon it, Aunt, she is enjoying herself in her own quiet style, and I know she's vastly obliged to you for all your kindness, as indeed I am myself."

But beneath the placid exterior which Phoebe presented to her relatives lay an increasing tension. She had many admirers, as was only to be expected, but her lack of response made several turn away to more promising quarry. One in particular, however, refused to be daunted. This was the highly eligible Viscount St. Keyne, who at seven and thirty years of age had for several years been abandoned as a hopeless aspiration by matchmaking mamas.

Lord St. Keyne was neither a Corinthian nor a dandy, yet he mingled among both sets, maintaining a reserve, however, which prevented his becoming intimate with either. It was known that from time to time he had had mistresses in keeping, but such affairs had been conducted discreetly, as became a man of rank with a position to uphold in the ton. He was of middle height with a distinguished rather than handsome countenance, dressed himself in the unostentatious but elegant style favoured by Beau Brummell, and was possessed of a considerable fortune.

His attentions to Phoebe had begun early in her visit, but until recently had not been noticed by the tattlemongers, because of the restraint he practised. During the past week, however, tongues had been busy, for he had found some way of being in her company almost every day. He was seen driving in the park with Lady Phoebe, paying morning calls at Lord

Eversley's house in Curzon Street, and keeping close to her side at balls and evening parties.

Eleanor could not resist teasing her friend a little over this when next they chanced to have an opportunity for a quiet little talk together.

"I declare, I have almost abandoned hope of ever finding you alone, my dear. A certain gentleman seems determined to dog your footsteps nowadays — he has quite routed all your other admirers, and now you haven't a single flirt left for your amusement."

Phoebe looked distressed. "You are joking, I know, Nell, for you're well aware that I don't wish to flirt with anyone."

"No, I suppose not, but it seems a pity. For my part, I quite enjoy a little harmless flirtation."

"Such as you share with Mr. Summers?" asked Phoebe, smiling. "Or is that more serious, Nell?"

"Gracious, no! I have no wish to be serious over anyone at present," replied Eleanor flippantly.

"I think Tom was becoming so over you, though," retorted her friend, with a challenging look.

Eleanor coloured. "Not he! He liked to fancy himself a little in love with me, but you can see for yourself how quickly it passed off, and now he is become the biggest flirt of them all. I believe Tom has a long way to go before he settles on any one female."

Phoebe nodded. "So Mama always said, and for once I agree with her. But truly, Nell —" her tone became more serious — "I am not at all happy at present. In fact, I would like to return home. I live in daily dread that Lord St. Keyne will declare himself, for although I hope you know me better than to think me conceited, I greatly fear that his attentions are serious. And so my aunt thinks. What am I to do?"

"Why, you have only to refuse him civilly but firmly," said Eleanor reasonably. "And if he applies to Tom, as he doubtless will do, you've told me that Tom is prepared to endorse your refusal. I don't see what there is to distress you in that. Of course, there is a certain embarrassment in such matters —"

"That's precisely what does distress me," replied Phoebe plaintively. "What reason can I give for a refusal? I cannot say that I am betrothed. I cannot think what to do! Nor do I place much reliance on Tom — he won't at all care to be obliged to refuse such an eligible suitor only on what must appear to be a sister's whim. It would be different altogether if Geoffrey and I were really betrothed."

"My love, you are making difficulties over nothing," said Eleanor gently. "It seems to me the simplest thing is merely to say that, much as you like and respect him, you cannot feel that degree of attachment to him which you consider an essential part of marriage. There! How does that sound?"

"Very well," admitted Phoebe. "But is there not a risk that he may persevere in order to change my feelings towards him?"

"Possibly, but that need not concern you too much. You'll be returning home in a month or so, I dare say."

"Yes, and that solves nothing," said Phoebe despondently. "Mama is still set on my marrying my cousin. She has kept hinting at it in every letter I receive from her. It seems that your attempt to disgust her with him achieved nothing, after all. It is too depressing!"

A change came over Eleanor's face. She realised suddenly that Mr. Eversley might not have been the only person to misinterpret her regrettable charade on Phoebe's behalf. Perhaps Lady Chalgrove, too, might have supposed that she was attempting to lead on Tom by representing his cousin as a rival. Not that she cared any more for Lady Chalgrove's opinion than she did for Frederick Eversley's. All the same, it was humiliating to be judged so undeservedly harshly. "My little plan certainly does seem to have misfired," she said, with an attempt at a nonchalant shrug. "The only person I've succeeded in bringing into disrepute seems to be myself."

"Why should you say so?" asked Phoebe, diverted from her previous theme by curiosity on this point. "Has Tom reproached you? Is that perhaps why he no longer shows a keen interest in you?"

"No such thing!" Eleanor forced a laugh. "Tom has never even raised the subject with me — I don't think he considered it important. He simply came to realise that we were too much on a brother and sister footing for any other relationship to be possible."

"But someone must have put that notion into your head," persisted Phoebe. "Was it Mama? Have you heard in a roundabout way of something she's said? I assure you she's never expressed any criticism of you to me."

"No, it was not your mother, though I couldn't help realising that evening how deeply she disapproved of my conduct. That is no new thing, however."

"Mama is prodigiously conventional, as you know, Nell," apologised Phoebe. "And lately I think her attitude towards you has changed because of Tom's interest in you. She never did approve of any girl whom Tom seemed to favour."

Eleanor nodded. She knew all this quite well.

"But if it wasn't either Tom or Mama, then who was it?" went on Phoebe, relentless in her quest for information on what was rapidly assuming the look of a mystery.

Eleanor hesitated, but she and Phoebe had been confidantes for too long to withhold secrets from each other. "Well, if you must know, it was your cousin, Mr. Eversley," she said, colouring in spite of herself.

"Freddy? What in the world can have possessed him?" asked Phoebe, in amazement. "He is always so vastly civil — besides, I have the impression that he likes you."

"I cannot imagine where you gained such a notion. It seems he thinks very poorly of me — more, possibly, than I deserve, though I'll admit I was foolish." She proceeded to explain the misunderstanding between them, while Phoebe listened sympathetically.

"Poor Nell! It is too bad that you should be so misjudged. How can anyone who has known you, even for a short time, possibly think that you are one of these man-hunting females? Such devices are beneath you. You've always been fond of making little plots, of course, but only to try and assist your friends," she added, recalling many past occasions when Eleanor had concocted madcap schemes to this end. "You would scorn to plot for your own advantage, especially in such a matter."

Eleanor laughed. "You are very loyal, my love, but you give me undue credit. Nevertheless, I'll admit I'm too proud to catch a husband. I hope to be sought after, rather than be obliged to do the seeking myself."

"Well, you certainly don't lack admirers, so you have only to fix upon one, and show him some encouragement," replied Phoebe. "But, oh, dear Nell —" she sighed heavily — "I wish I knew what I could do in my present situation."

Eleanor dragged her straying thoughts back from the unexpected path they were following as a result of her friend's first remark. "As I see it, your only recourse is to force Tom into taking a stand with your mama," she said firmly. "If he gives his consent to your marriage with Geoffrey Lydhurst, she must yield. Now that he's about to go against her wishes in the matter of procuring a residence in town, it should be possible to urge him to assert his authority on your behalf. Do try, Phoebe."

Phoebe promised she would, though with little conviction. Fond though she was of her brother, she was not blind to his faults, one of which was to evade unpleasant issues whenever possible.

As it transpired, Phoebe did not need to broach the subject with Tom, for he introduced it himself at the first opportunity of their being alone together.

"I want a word with you, Phoebe," he said peremptorily, a scowl on his handsome face. "A fine mess you've made of things, my girl! Here's St. Keyne just asked my permission to pay his addresses to you, and I didn't know how to answer the fellow."

Phoebe turned pale and clasped both hands over her bosom. "But — but, Tom —" she stammered. "You know you promised to refuse anyone who came to you — oh, you did send him away, didn't you? You did leave him in no doubt of my answer? I should die of mortification were he to propose to me."

Tom had the grace to look a little shamefaced. "Well, I know I said I'd refuse any suitors for your hand, but the thing is, 'tis a difficult business with a man like St. Keyne — a fellow who's well up in the ton! How can I defer a highly eligible parti whom most girls would give anything to catch in their net? 'Tis all very well talking of doing it, but when it comes to the point, it's jolly tricky, I can tell you."

His sister turned even paler than before. "So what did you say to him?" she asked, in a strained whisper.

He avoided her agonised gaze, shuffling his feet like a guilty schoolboy. "I did the best I could," he muttered awkwardly. "Told him that of course there could be no possible objection to him on my side, but that you would be the one to make the ultimate decision. Well, what else could I do?" he burst out, half-frightened by her look of panic. "Couldn't insult a man of his standing by giving him a categorical denial. Show some sense, Phoebe, do, for heaven's sake."

She returned no answer, but rose hurriedly and almost ran from the room, while her brother stood staring after her.

"Females!" he exclaimed, in tones of deep disgust. "No use in trying to knock any sense into their heads."

CHAPTER XI

Eleanor and her sister had just finished breakfasting together on the following morning, Viscount Pamyngton having left the house earlier, when one of the footmen came in with a note which had been delivered by hand.

"For me?" said Eleanor in surprise, as she accepted it from him. "Now, who on earth — ah, I see! It's from Phoebe — though why she should write to me, instead of calling —" Her voice tailed off as she opened the missive and began to read its contents. It was written in a hastily scrawled hand with several blots and crossings-out, quite unlike her friend's usual elegant style. She had read no more than a few lines when she let out a dismayed exclamation.

"What is it?" asked Catherine, with the liveliest curiosity. "Is anything amiss with Phoebe — or Tom?"

"Hush!" replied Eleanor, waving an imperative hand at her. "I'll tell you in a minute."

Thus adjured, Katie obediently fell silent, gleaning what information she could from her sister's eloquent expressions, which varied from dismay and pity to fierce indignation.

"Well!" exclaimed Eleanor, when she had finished reading and screwed the note up into a ball which she clenched in an indignant fist. "If that isn't just like Tom. Of all the cowardly, mean, despicable —" Words failed her as she jumped to her feet. "And so I shall tell him," she said viciously, "without losing another moment. Katie, may I borrow the carriage? I must go at once to Curzon Street."

"Why, yes, but pray tell me what it is all about," protested Katie. "You cannot just go off, leaving me in the dark."

"'Tis poor Phoebe — oh, I know she's a goose, but she is my friend, and she can't help her nature. You remember I told you of the attachment between her and Geoffrey Lydhurst?"

Katie nodded.

"The thing is that Viscount St. Keyne has been pursuing her lately, as you may have observed, and she's been terrified that he would declare himself and she'd be faced with the ordeal of refusing him. She was counting on the fact that he would first ask Tom's permission to address her, and Tom had promised her faithfully before she came to London that he would deflect any serious suitors. He knew all about Lydhurst, you see. But what has he done, do you suppose?"

Katie shook her head dumbly, knowing the question to be rhetorical.

"Why, taken his usual weak-kneed attitude," stormed Eleanor, "and sent St. Keyne to Phoebe for his answer. Just wait until I see him, and he'll wish himself elsewhere."

"But are you sure that you should interfere?" asked her sister dubiously. "'Tis between Tom and Phoebe, after all, Nell."

"When Phoebe has fled from home rather than face St. Keyne?" demanded Eleanor.

"She's what?" gasped Katie.

"Yes, she says so here. She wrote this last night, and was planning to leave early this morning, before the household was astir — and by stage coach, too, since she wished to avoid having a chaise call for her at the house."

"Oh, dear heavens! What must Lady Eversley think? Say what you will, Nell, Phoebe Chalgrove is a silly girl."

"She's very timid," excused Eleanor. "But that's another reason for my going to Curzon Street. She asks me to explain matters to her aunt, since she felt quite unequal to the task herself. Just wait until I get my hands on Tom, though!"

Perhaps fortunately, this proved impossible when she arrived hurriedly at the Eversleys' house shortly afterwards, for Lady Eversley, admirably concealing her surprise at so early a morning call, informed her that Thomas had left some time previously with a party of friends, and was not expected back until the following day.

"Do you know where he was bound, ma'am?" asked Eleanor, thwarted of her prey.

"Oh, some sporting occasion, I believe," was the reply, "but precisely what or where, I didn't trouble to enquire. I am sorry that Phoebe should not yet be downstairs to receive you," Lady Eversley went on. "The child was unwell yesterday evening, and said she did not wish to be disturbed, so I haven't sent up to her room as yet, though I was just about to do so. We must send for the doctor if she's no better, though she insisted it was nothing but a headache brought on by fatigue."

This was Eleanor's cue to explain matters, which she proceeded to do to an accompaniment of incredulous exclamations from her hostess.

"The foolish child!" the latter said, at the end of this recital. "Why could she not confide in me? I might have been able to find some way out of the tangle. But to run back home without a word spoken —"

"She is very much aware of the awkward situation in which she's placed you," excused Eleanor. "She feared you might attempt to persuade her to remain if she confided in you, and she was by far too panic-stricken to know quite what she was doing. Poor Phoebe! I blame her brother. He has behaved abominably, and I can't wait to tell him so."

"As to that, I have no notion where he may be, though Frederick may know. Oh dear, it is all so difficult. And I suppose I shall be obliged to manufacture some excuse for her absence, since she has several engagements for the coming weeks. Of course, I have it!" she exclaimed, her brow lightening. "I shall say that my sister has been taken ill and wants Phoebe at home. And I must say," she added with a touch of acerbity, "that I do not feel at all in charity with Ianthe — Lady Chalgrove — at present! She should never have forced my niece to come to town against her will. I know she had some stupid notion in her head that Phoebe and my son Frederick — however, I've hinted to her more than once that such a scheme is absurd. Freddy has no interest at all in marriage, more's the pity, for I do think a family life gives one stability. However, young people will go their own way, and so Ianthe must learn, I fear."

Having delivered her message, Eleanor felt there was nothing to detain her longer, so took a friendly leave of Lady Eversley and was shown out of the house. As she walked down the steps towards her waiting carriage, a curricle pulled up behind it and the driver, tossing the reins to his groom, jumped down.

She recognised Frederick Eversley and hailed him at once. He bowed.

"Good morning, Miss Denham."

"Mr. Eversley," she began without preamble, "do you know where your cousin Chalgrove is?"

He looked surprised at the direct question, but answered readily enough. "I was half-expecting to find him indoors myself, but since you've just emerged from the house, ma'am, evidently he's not."

She shook her head impatiently. "No, Lady Eversley's just told me that he left earlier with a party of friends, bound for some sporting occasion. She also said that you might know exactly where, so pray tell me if you do, for 'tis of the utmost importance to me."

He regarded her gravely. "You seem a trifle put out, ma'am," he said, after a moment's hesitation. "Is there any way in which I can serve you?"

"Indeed there is — by telling me at once where Tom can be found, so that I can go after him," she replied brusquely.

"You'll scarce do that — he's gone to Crawley to see a prize fight," he said drily. "I'm just off there myself, as a matter of fact. I was going to take him up if he hadn't already gone with someone else."

"You mean boxing?" She looked daunted for a moment, but soon rallied. "No matter — my business with him can't wait, so I must follow him. But I can't keep my sister's coach all day, so I'll send back a message with the coachman, and hire a vehicle."

"Follow him — to a *fight*!" expostulated the Honourable Frederick. "You must be out of your mind, Miss Denham! I've no wish to pry into your personal concerns, of course, but surely there's nothing which can't wait until he returns here tomorrow."

"I tell you there is," she said tartly. "And if you will have the goodness to offer me a seat in your vehicle as far as the nearest coach hire office, I'll endeavour to explain."

By now, he was not only alive with curiosity, but also experiencing various other, more unpleasant sensations. It began to look very much as though Eleanor Denham had changed her mind, and was now set on becoming a countess, after all. Why else should she urgently wish to pursue Tom?

Whatever her reasons, he decided at once that he must dissuade her from this headstrong plan, and probably the simplest way of doing so was to fall in with her wishes for the moment. He expressed his readiness to drive her to the coach office and waited while she gave her coachman a message for her sister.

"I didn't wish to be driven to the office by Pamyngton's coachman," she explained as she allowed him to assist her into the curricle, "otherwise Katie will learn of it and become alarmed. I've told her I'm going for a drive with you, which is true, after all."

Freddy nodded, intent on hearing the reason behind all this, yet half-fearing what the explanation might be. She soon began, and his relief was so considerable on hearing her story that he failed to feel the compassion for his cousin Phoebe which Miss Denham evidently expected to arouse in him.

"What a stupid chit!" he exclaimed in disgust. "To run away, and by stage coach — stage coach, I ask you! Did she take a maid with her?"

"I'm not quite certain, but I rather think not, or Lady Eversley would have known of it," Eleanor replied. "Still, 'tis no matter. I am not taking one with me now."

"You may think 'tis no matter, but I disagree," he said forthrightly. "Moreover, what can you possibly hope to achieve by getting hold of Tom? His sister's gone, and there's an end to it. He can't stop her now."

Eleanor glared at him. "What he can do — and will do, if I can find any means to compel him — is to follow her home and take a firm stand with Lady Chalgrove over Phoebe's future. He must go at once. That poor girl can't be left in misery any longer."

He digested this for a moment in silence, skilfully manoeuvring his curricle through the traffic. "I'll tell you what," he said suddenly, "I'll go after Tom and bring him back to see you. Allow me to drive you home now."

She shook her head. "No, that won't do. He won't come back for you, I know, and then there'll be two days wasted. I must speak with him myself as soon as possible, and shame him into returning home immediately. Say no more —" as he started to interrupt — "I am *quite* determined."

"In that case," he said, in a resigned tone, "permit me to offer to drive you down to Crawley myself — though, heaven knows, the town will be Bedlam with a fight taking place, and not fit for a lady. However, it will be preferable to your going there unescorted in a hired vehicle."

"Oh, would you indeed?" She turned a radiant face towards him. "That would be so kind of you. And no doubt you'll reach there much faster with your kind of horses," she added, with an admiring glance at his matched bays.

"Yes, but I shan't flog them to death," he replied. "We'll make a change at Croydon and again at Horley — I'm known at both posting inns, and can rely on getting the best."

"Perhaps I ought not to involve you in my concerns," she said with belated contrition, as he headed towards Westminster Bridge.

"They're my family concerns, too, aren't they?" he said cheerfully. "Besides, I was going to Crawley on my own account — that's if the fight isn't over by the time we reach there. I was later starting than I intended."

She made no reply to this; and, indeed, there was little opportunity for conversation as they made their way through London's heavy traffic. Later, when they came on to the highway, and their pace increased, the presence of the groom inhibited all but the most commonplace remarks.

From time to time, each cast a covert appraising glance at the other. Freddy was thinking how attractive his passenger looked in her lilac pelisse and the saucy bonnet trimmed with ribbons of the same delicate shade. For her part, Eleanor noted with approval his skilful handling of the horses and reflected how comfortable it was to be travelling with someone who, whatever his faults, did manage to inspire her with a feeling of confidence.

The change of horses at Croydon delayed them less than ten minutes, and it was little more than an hour later when they pulled up outside the Chequers Inn at Horley. This was always a busy posting house, but today there seemed more bustle than usual, with groups of people standing about among the carriages in the forecourt, and ostlers dashing to and fro. In no time at all, however, three or four of the latter presented themselves to the Honourable Frederick's groom, who had swung himself down from the rear seat, prepared to handle matters.

"It occurs to me, Miss Denham, that you may like to enter the inn for a few minutes and partake of some refreshment," said Freddy, holding out his hand to assist Eleanor to dismount. "I'm bound to admit, I'm parched myself."

"Well, if we're not too long," she temporised.

"Heavens, ma'am, we're only a matter of five miles or so from Crawley, and Tom isn't likely to run away while a fight's in progress," he reassured her.

This seemed reasonable enough, so she allowed him to help her out of the curricle and lead her into a pleasant, half-timbered inn. The landlord came forward at once to greet

Frederick, who was a well-known and honoured customer, making his way with difficulty through the crowded hall.

"Business pretty brisk today, Newton," commented Freddy.

"Yes, your honour," agreed the man. "What with the prize fight over at Crawley, and one of the stage coaches broken down and all the passengers kicking their heels in the house, we're in a fair old turmoil. But what's your pleasure, Mr. Eversley — what can I bring ye?"

Freddy was about to answer when a startled exclamation escaped Eleanor, who had been busy looking about her.

"Phoebe!" she cried. "Of all things!"

"Nell — oh, Nell!" echoed a voice from amid the crowd standing nearby. "I'm so glad to see you here." The next moment Phoebe had darted forward and flung herself into her friend's arms.

The Honourable Frederick had never been inclined to play out dramatic scenes in public, and he could see with half an eye that one such eventuality was imminent. With great presence of mind, therefore, he requested a private parlour, and quickly steered the two young ladies into this refuge. "Now," he said, having ordered some refreshment and settled them comfortably side by side on a window seat, "squawk as much as you like."

"How very odious you are," reproved Nell, though her eyes were dancing. "But never mind him, Phoebe — tell me how you come to be here instead of travelling towards home. I was never so surprised in my life as to see you."

"It was the stage coach. The wretched thing broke down a few miles from here, and we were all obliged to walk to this inn," explained Phoebe. "And, Nell, I wasn't sure what I could do, for I've very little money with me, and couldn't possibly find enough to hire another vehicle to take me the rest of the way. I was in despair when you and my cousin arrived, wondering how I might contrive, for Mama is not known here, and I wasn't at all confident that the landlord would trust me for the fee. I was never more thankful in my life to see someone I knew."

"You shouldn't have run off in the first place, you know," said Freddy severely. "Sorry to say this, Phoebe, but it was a stupid thing to do."

"How dare you scold her!" reproved Nell. "You know well it is all Tom's fault. Not," she added, addressing Phoebe in a milder tone, "that I don't think you'd have done better to stay and explain matters to Lady Eversley, then perhaps she would have dismissed St. Keyne for you. She is a very understanding person, unlike some members of her family." She gave Freddy a sidelong, provocative glance, but he merely grinned in response.

"I do feel I have indeed treated my aunt badly," confessed Phoebe, in a doleful tone, "after all her great kindness to me. I did not stop to think at the time — I was too upset — but how will she explain matters to all those who have invited me to this and that occasion? How can I ever face her again?"

"Don't distress yourself," advised Freddy kindly. "My mother is equal to anything — bound to be, after bringing up two such harum-scarum chits as my sisters. She'll concoct some excuse — illness in the family, I dare say."

"Precisely what she had decided upon before I left her," said Nell.

He nodded. "What do you intend to do now?" he asked. "Are you still determined to return home, Phoebe?"

"Yes, I must go, although I realise it solves nothing, for Mama will never agree to a betrothal between Geoffrey and myself," she answered despondently. "She is too set on another match for me."

"Something already in mind, has she?" asked Freddy curiously.

Phoebe blushed.

"Oh, you may as well tell him," said Nell impulsively. "If you must know, Mr. Eversley, Phoebe's mother was hoping that you two would marry."

Freddy started. "What? Well, I'll be —" He drew a deep breath and refrained from finishing the sentence. "If that isn't too much!" he declared disgustedly. "'Tis bad enough having matchmaking mamas on one's track in town, without having to contend with it in the bosom of one's own family. Yes, and now I come to think of it, my mother may have known something of this, for I gained a distinct impression that she was keeping something back when first she suggested I should accompany her to Chalgrove Park. Wait until I see her!"

"I am so very sorry," said Phoebe humbly, still blushing. "I trust you realise that I had no part in such a scheme — indeed, how could I, when my whole happiness is bound up in another?"

"No, of course not. And I trust you understand that there's nothing personal in my attitude," said Freddy placatingly. "'Tis simply that I'm a confirmed old bachelor." He paused for a moment, looking thoughtful, then suddenly continued with a twinkle in his eye. "Or at least, I was. But, yes, by Jove, Phoebe, I think you can put a stop to any ideas my aunt may have on that score by telling her that I'm about to become engaged to another lady. If she'll have me, that is," he added dubiously.

Phoebe's face brightened. "Oh, truly? How splendid! That will certainly remove one obstacle from my path. I do wish you happy, Freddy, most sincerely."

"Well, as to that, I cannot be sure," he said cautiously. "But we shall see."

Eleanor had been attending to this conversation with intense interest, but now she saw fit to interrupt it. "I'll remove the other obstacle for you, Phoebe. I must and will talk to Tom at once. He is at Crawley on some sporting occasion, and Mr. Eversley was taking me to him when we chanced on you. I don't quite know how we may contrive, though, for you cannot come with us, and I won't leave you here alone."

"The easiest thing is for you two ladies to remain here and I'll bring Tom to you," said Freddy, rising and picking up his hat and gloves. "It may be some time before we're back, but I'll order some food to be brought in to you."

"Oh, very well," agreed Eleanor, while Phoebe brightened visibly at the thought that she need no longer decide matters for herself. "But if you mean to leave us alone here for hours while you watch your odious boxing match, I may warn you now that you will have a stormy reception on your return."

"You put me all in a tremble, ma'am," Freddy answered, with a mocking look. "But I'll do my best to bring my cousin back straightaway, though it may not be easy."

In the event, it was more than two hours later before he ushered an indignant Tom into the parlour of the Chequers.

"What's to do?" he demanded of his sister. "Freddy tells me that you've behaved like a perfect idiot, running away from my aunt and upsetting everyone. Let me tell you, my girl —"

"And let me tell *you*," interrupted Eleanor furiously, "that you are to blame for everything. Had Phoebe been able to rely upon you for the protection you promised her, she would never have felt so desperate that only flight seemed possible."

He raked her with a scathing look. "I fail to see, Miss Denham, what concern this is of yours."

"Do you indeed? Poor Phoebe may not possess a brother who cares a jot for her happiness, but she has one friend, at least, who is determined to defend her interests."

"Very neat," murmured Freddy approvingly. "Well put, Miss Denham."

"Mind your own business!" directed his cousin. Then, turning to Eleanor, "I would like to point out to you, ma'am, that this is a family matter."

"However much you may call me 'Miss Denham' and 'ma'am', you cannot do away with the fact that we have all grown up together, and are almost as one family," retorted Nell hotly. "And I say that someone needs to tell you that you've treated your sister abominably, since she herself is by far too sweet-natured to say so."

"A disadvantage from which you evidently do not suffer, ma'am!"

"Oh, I say — a facer," put in Freddy, grinning.

"Will you hold your tongue?" directed Tom, turning an angry look upon him.

"You may insult me as much as you choose," went on Nell, ignoring the interruption. "In fact, I'm glad of it, for it enables me to tell you to your face that I consider you the most cowardly —"

"Tut, tut. A vicious accusation, but understandable in the heat of the moment," remarked Freddy, who was plainly enjoying himself.

"Be quiet, Mr. Eversley! This is no occasion for facetiousness," Nell threw at him. "What I was saying, Tom, is that I find your behaviour craven in the extreme. I —"

"Now, by heaven, you've gone too far, ma'am. I won't listen to you anymore —"

"Oh, yes, you will! It is high time you played the man and showed Lady Chalgrove that you are head of the household. And if no one else will inform you of this, then I must and shall. *You* can give Phoebe permission to marry whomsoever she chooses, so why don't you assert yourself for once? How can you have the heart to stand by and see her suffer, only for the lack of a modicum of resolution on your part? You should be monstrously ashamed!"

For a few moments, Tom was rendered speechless at this outspoken attack, while feelings of outrage struggled with an inescapable conviction of guilt. Phoebe seized the respite to attempt a reconciliation.

"Tom, dearest, pray don't fall out with Nell," she pleaded, catching his arm. "We've been friends all our lives, the three of us, and though perhaps she expresses herself a trifle forthrightly, she means only to help. Just as she tried to help me once before when she said all those outrageous things concerning Freddy —"

The two young men looked at each other, then back at Phoebe.

"What outrageous things?" demanded Tom.

"Surely you recall that evening at home before we came to London, when Nell dined with us, and she tried to make out that she and Freddy had been — well — particular friends some years before, in Brighton?"

"Oh, that," replied Tom, regarding his cousin with a grin. "Yes, indeed I remember. Freddy gave it as his opinion that Nell had a taste for melodrama. Not sure he isn't right about it, either," he added darkly, "judging by her present performance."

Nell greeted this with lofty disdain.

"The truth was," continued Phoebe hesitantly, "that she was exaggerating in order to set Mama against my cousin. You see, I had confided to Nell that Mama was hoping Freddy and I —" She broke off, confused.

Frederick laughed, a feeling of euphoria taking possession of him as light suddenly dawned. "I dare say you're not aware, Tom, that my aunt has a plan to pair off Phoebe and myself? I realise now that Miss Denham's talented performance that evening was calculated to show me up in my true colours as an unworthy partner. A noble gesture, you must admit."

"So that was it. I must say, it's all of a piece with Nell's hare-brained schemes," said Tom, in a more friendly tone than he had used so far.

"Well, whatever you may think of it, she was doing the only thing she could think of to assist me," retorted Phoebe warmly. "She has always been the truest of friends. I don't wish to vex you, Tom," she went on, in a conciliatory tone, "but I can't help feeling that Nell is right in saying that the time has come for you to make Mama realise that you are head of the house. You won't wish to hurt her feelings, any more than I do, but perhaps she could be persuaded to it — gently, you know, but firmly."

"That's all very well," began Tom, then broke off on meeting Eleanor's contemptuous look. He squared his shoulders. "Well, I'll have a go at it. Grimmond has just found me a capital town house in Albemarle Street, and I'll have to break that news to Mama, so I may as well go the whole hog, while I'm about it, and settle your future. Mind, it'll be an uncomfortable business."

Frederick nodded. "Just so, and I've always found, old chap, that anything of that nature is best tackled straightaway." He looked at his watch. "You're only fifteen miles or so from Chalgrove Park, so why don't you take your sister there now? My mother's giving family illness as an excuse for Phoebe's absence. So the same will serve for you. Any particular messages I'll be happy to deliver for you, of course, as I'm returning to town immediately."

"Excellent notion," approved Tom. "I'll see the landlord about hiring a chaise."

"What will you do, Nell?" asked Phoebe, as he rose to set about this. "Will you return with my cousin?"

"Only too happy —" began Freddy, but Eleanor cut him short.

"Thank you, but I, too, shall return home for a few days," she said, with a frigid glance at him. "Tom, if you will have the goodness to hire a vehicle to accommodate the three of us, I'll go with you and Phoebe."

He assented, and went out of the parlour.

"And then I can keep him up to scratch," said Nell to Phoebe, with a conspiratorial look.

"Oh, yes, I'm sure you are wise. But what of your sister, dearest? Will she not expect you back in Hanover Square?"

"Yes, of course, so I must get word to her," replied Nell. "I'll write a note, and perhaps —" She hesitated, looking somewhat awkwardly at Freddy as she realised that, little though she felt in charity with him at the moment, she must ask a favour of him.

He saw her predicament and promptly came to her aid with a mischievous look in his eye. "Happy to deliver it for you, ma'am — easiest thing in the world to look in on Lady Pamyngton when I reach town."

"Thank you," she said stiffly. "And I must thank you, too, for conveying me here and fetching Tom to us. I fear it interfered with your original plan of seeing the sporting contest."

Inwardly, he cursed himself for ever having voiced to her his interpretation of her conduct on that fateful evening at Chalgrove Park. Phoebe had reminded her of it, and that was why she was so stiff with him now. However, the mischief was done, and he must do his best to please her now. "Delighted to be of service," he said amiably. "As a matter of fact, we did stay to see the last few rounds. All the same, I've seen a livelier fight here between you and Tom, I give you my word, ma'am!"

CHAPTER XII

The first few weeks after her family's departure for London were among the most miserable of Lady Chalgrove's existence. For many years, her every thought had been devoted to the welfare of her children and plans for their future; now all at once she found herself living in a void.

At first, she attempted to divert her energies into the management of the estate, and spent long hours closeted with Mellor in the office, or driving about with him. She made many suggestions for alterations or improvements, but although he always listened to her respectfully, he invariably ended by replying that he would certainly discuss it with his lordship on his return.

This gave rise to several urgent letters to Tom pointing out that he should return home as soon as possible, as nothing could be settled in his absence. The dutiful, if perfunctory, replies she received brought her no satisfaction. It was evident that Tom was enjoying himself far too much to contemplate an early return home, and, moreover, he was confident that all could safely be left in Mellor's competent hands.

She received an unpleasant shock when she learned that Eleanor Denham was also in London. She redoubled her appeals to her son, not forgetting to mention that she feared her health was suffering as a result of having the whole responsibility of the estate resting on her frail shoulders. This only resulted in an anxious letter from Phoebe offering to return home herself, an outcome which Lady Chalgrove certainly did not desire. She decided to abandon that tactic.

Other letters from Phoebe proved disappointing. All her mama's hints about the desirability of a union with her cousin — though Lady Chalgrove was careful never to go beyond hinting on this subject — produced no satisfactory response. Phoebe seldom mentioned Frederick, and when she did, it was only in the most casual, detached way. There was no suggestion from Lady Eversley, either, that her son had fallen captive to his young cousin's exceptional beauty. She told of Phoebe's other admirers, of whom there were plenty, but this was no more than Ianthe Chalgrove had anticipated, and was a matter of indifference to her. All she desired to hear was that her nephew and Phoebe were forming an attachment.

Her lifelong habit of never becoming intimate with any of her neighbours had deprived her of the comfort of a female confidante, so she had to turn to the tried and trusted man who had befriended her and her family for so many years. Lord Ashcroft looked in on her almost every day, and did his best to dispel her doubts with his usual kindly common sense.

"Mellor has become so difficult," she complained to him on one occasion. "I have made several suggestions for measures which might be taken in estate matters, but he will do nothing now without Tom's consent. It is so absurd. I have been used to giving him instructions myself until quite recently, when I judged that Tom should himself begin to assume his responsibilities."

"You were quite right in that, my dear Ianthe, and you can hardly be surprised that your agent has become accustomed to referring everything to Tom, as a result."

"No, but in his absence, surely Mellor should pay heed to me," she persisted, with a petulant air.

"I'm sure he does, but he'll feel more comfortable if he has Tom's confirmation," replied Ashcroft reasonably. "I dare say there's nothing which can't wait until Tom returns, is there?"

"Well, perhaps not, but oh, Harry, it makes me feel so useless," she said, the tears starting in her lovely blue eyes. "With my family from home, I scarce know how to occupy myself most of the time. It casts me into utter dejection!"

"Well, we can't have that," he answered in a rallying tone. "If you want occupation, I wonder if I might venture to suggest — but no, I dare say you would find it too much exertion," he added, glancing tenderly at her forlorn expression.

She gave him a half curious, half wary look. "What have you in mind?" she asked. "If it is some charitable enterprise, such as Lady Lyncroft undertakes, I fear that, much as I should like to take part in such worthy work, my constitution would never permit me to do so."

"No, no," he replied with a laugh. "Not unless you would count me a charitable enterprise."

She started, wondering where this might be leading, and fluttered her eyelashes at him. "What can you mean, Harry?"

But Lord Ashcroft was by far too old a hand to rush his fences in that way. "Why, simply that my housekeeper has been badgering me for nigh on a year to do something about refurbishing the Court," he said, in an easy tone. "For my part, I think it does well enough for an old bachelor like myself, but Mrs. Harris has her own notions on the subject, and she's been with me for so long I've no wish to come to blows with her. I've considered leaving it all to her, for such matters need a woman's touch. I'm no judge of what's fashionable in the way of decor and so on. But if I could possibly prevail upon you, my dear Ianthe, to give us both the benefit of your excellent taste, I'm sure the old house could be made to look much more stylish."

Her face lit up at once, for this was a scheme which offered scope for her considerable artistic talent. There was nothing of the kind that needed to be done in her own home at present; moreover, it would serve to give her thoughts a new direction.

"Am I presuming too much on our friendship?" he asked, with a diffidence which she could not help but find endearing. "Would it take up too much of your time?"

"Not at all," she responded eagerly. "My dear Harry, it is the very thing for me at present, when I find time hanging a trifle heavy on my hands. Besides, I should like to assist you as some small return for the many kindnesses you have shown over the years to myself and my dear family." A warm, melting glance accompanied these words, and almost disturbed the gentleman's composure.

"Come now," he said brusquely, to cover his emotion. "One doesn't measure friendship in terms of receipts and payments. But are you quite sure you won't find it tedious?"

She reassured him once more, and he was satisfied. After all, he had made the suggestion solely for her benefit. It was true that his housekeeper had from time to time advocated changes at Staplewood Court, but there had been no urgency and small hope of a result in her representations. Now, however, he could turn this circumstance to good use, gratifying both Ianthe Chalgrove and himself. It would create a diversion for the lady, and give him the inestimable pleasure not only of her company, but also of watching her transform his house into the kind of home it might have been had she chosen to grace it as mistress. He drove her over there in his phaeton the very next day, and conducted her from room to room with Mrs. Harris in attendance. Of course, Lady Chalgrove knew the house well, but she had always taken it for granted, in the way one does when a place has been familiar for years. Now she looked at everything with fresh eyes, seeing much that was old-fashioned or even downright shabby, and marvelling that she had never before noticed such faults.

Staplewood Court had been built by Lord Ashcroft's ancestors in the seventeenth century, and much of the original interior remained as it had then been. In 1750, however, his grandfather had carried out a certain amount of modernisation, removing oak panelling from the hall, dining-room and the principal bedrooms to substitute plastered walls which could then be decorated in light pastel shades after the latest fashion.

For some reason now obscure, the panelling in the drawing-room still remained, darkened by age and giving a heavy look to the room which was accentuated by the old-fashioned mahogany furniture. Lady Chalgrove paused on the threshold, looking critically about her for the first time, and shook her head decidedly.

"Oh dear, I fear something needs to be done in here, do you not agree, Harry?"

"I must say, it looks well enough to me," he replied, looking round with proprietary eyes and failing to find anything wanting. "However, if you think it dowdy, Ianthe, we'll have it seen to. What do you suggest?"

She pondered for a while. "It needs lightening," she said at last. "I think perhaps all that dark oak should be replaced."

"'Tis fine panelling, done by a master craftsman," he put in, obviously reluctant to see it go.

"Well, perhaps we could keep it," she conceded, "but it does give a heavy look to the room. I know!" she exclaimed, as an inspiration struck her. "Why should we not have it painted white? And then, you know, if we replaced those lattice windows, which admit so little light, with a handsome bow giving a wide view of the gardens, and replaced the furniture with something in the modern style, rosewood, say, with striped satin seats, and a few comfortable wing armchairs —"

She continued for some time in this way, while Lord Ashcroft watched her animated countenance and thought the sacrifice of his familiar furnishings a small price to pay for giving his lady love so much pleasure.

"Oh, yes, milady!" enthused the housekeeper. "Indeed, that would transform the room."

"Of course, we would need new hangings," continued Lady Chalgrove, fingering the heavy, slightly faded velvet curtains. "These do well enough for the present decor, but will scarcely fit our new scheme. Do you not agree, Harry?"

He agreed, both to this and to every other improvement she suggested, stipulating only that his library should remain unchanged. As Lady Chalgrove never passed any length of time in such places, not being of a bookish turn of mind, she was quite content to reserve her talents for more interesting areas.

The succeeding weeks passed agreeably for them both, with almost daily meetings. There were consultations with the architect and builders, painters and craftsmen, in all of which Lady Chalgrove shared. She had come to feel that her opinion counted for little in the running of her own estate at Chalgrove Park, so it was refreshing to discover how greatly it was valued at Staplewood Court.

Her letters to her family became less frequent and demanding as her interest in the new project grew. While she was so agreeably occupied, it no longer seemed urgent that

Tom should return home, and she had little time to spare for brooding over Phoebe's concerns.

This euphoric state of mind received a severe set-back, however, when she opened a letter from her sister one morning. She read it through twice over breakfast, then retired, considerably agitated, to a sheltered seat in the garden, where lilacs blossomed in the warm May sunshine.

It was here that Lord Ashcroft found her brooding half an hour later, when he called to drive her over to Staplewood Court, now in the throes of its transformation.

She heard his step on the paved path leading to her retreat, and looked up at him with a woebegone face. He could see that she had been weeping, although in spite of this she still contrived to look lovely, unlike the majority of females, he reflected.

"My dear Ianthe, whatever is amiss?" he exclaimed in concern. Seeing the letter in her right hand, he sat down beside her and took her free hand in his. "Bad news?" he asked gently. "Tom? Or Phoebe? Tell me, if you feel equal to it."

She turned tearful blue eyes up to him, clinging to his hand. He tightened his grip reassuringly and waited for her to speak.

"The end of all my hopes," she whispered after a moment, in an infinitely sad voice.

His face paled a little under its tan. "Good heavens! Do you mean — an accident to one of them — to both?"

She shook her head. "Not that, no. They are well enough."

He drew a deep breath of relief. Whatever else it was, at least it could not be too bad. Females were emotional creatures, after all, he told himself.

"Nevertheless, they are both lost to me," she continued, in a histrionic tone, "if what Anne writes here —" she waved the letter — "should come to pass."

"No, no, it can't be as bad as all that," he said comfortingly. "Suppose you tell me the whole?"

"It's bad enough," she insisted tearfully. "To begin with, Tom has set about purchasing a house in town. My sister says that Grimmond — our lawyer, you know — has found a suitable one in Albemarle Street, and the business is all but settled. And not one word to me from Tom about it! One might have supposed," she went on, misery giving way to indignation, "that his own mother would at least have been consulted. But no, he arranges all without a by-your-leave, and has not even the common courtesy to inform me himself, but allows me to hear it first from my sister. It is not to be borne, after all I have done for him!"

Ashcroft coughed awkwardly, for he understood well why Tom had not told his mother of his intention. The difficulty was how to explain this to her. "I dare say, my dear Ianthe, that he thought you might raise objections to the scheme — as, indeed, you have done previously."

"So he deliberately goes against my known wishes?" There was anger in her voice now.

"Don't blame him too much. He wouldn't be the first young man to shirk a contentious issue. I must remind you again, I fear, little though I wish to vex you —"

"— that Tom is his own master," she said petulantly. "Thank you, Harry, you've already told me so a score of times!" She snatched her hand away and turned from him.

"And I must do so another score if need be, in the name of friendship," he replied in a firm tone. "'Tis a fact you must come to terms with, Ianthe, if you wish to maintain a loving relationship with your son. He's a man, not a boy any longer."

She made no answer to this, but brooded in silence for a few moments. Almost he expected a summary dismissal; then she spoke again. "And then there's Phoebe," she continued in a despondent tone. "Anne writes that one Viscount St. Keyne — do you know the man? — is paying his addresses, and she thinks perhaps Phoebe may accept him. So I shall lose her, too."

"St. Keyne," he repeated. "Yes, I think I've run across him when I've been in town. He's no end of a catch, you know — title, flourishing estate, wealth. If you want a brilliant match for little Phoebe, you couldn't do better, I'd say."

"But his estate's in Northumberland!" she wailed. "How often would I see my child if she were banished to such a distant spot? And I had planned that she should marry her cousin Frederick, because he's family, and we'd be meeting frequently on that account. Besides, when he marries he will need to purchase a country property, and there is Oakwood Hall, you know, on the market. Oh dear, it's none of it working out as I wished."

"As to that, plans seldom do. But I'll be surprised, I must confess, if Phoebe accepts St. Keyne, in spite of anything your sister may think."

Lady Chalgrove turned towards him again, with hope in her eyes. "Why, what can you mean? Do you suppose Frederick — "

Ashcroft shook his head decidedly, breaking in upon her. "Not young Eversley. I'd say neither of those two has the faintest interest in the other. But by all I saw before she went to town, a strong attachment already exists between Phoebe and Lydhurst's boy."

"Geoffrey Lydhurst?" She pondered for a moment. "Of course, it's not what I'd have liked," she said slowly. "But still, it would be preferable to St. Keyne and living in Northumberland. And I'm bound to admit that my sister has never encouraged me to think there were any hopes of Frederick — nor does Phoebe ever write of him with more than cousinly friendship, when she mentions him at all, that is. I don't know —"

"Interesting thing," remarked Ashcroft casually. "I was dining with the Lydhursts the other evening, and Lydhurst mentioned that he'd thought of purchasing Oakwood Hall for Geoffrey, as the boy would need an establishment of his own if he decided to wed."

Lady Chalgrove turned a radiant face upon him. "Did he indeed? Well, that would certainly seem — yet I don't know," she finished doubtfully.

"You've nothing against young Lydhurst, have you?"

"Oh, no. He's a very well-behaved young man and a great friend of Tom's, of course. The Lydhursts are an old family, too. Yes, I suppose it would do well enough," she acknowledged. "And better by far than having my daughter removed to some outlandish home in the North. But oh, Harry!" She sighed deeply.

"Still troubled, my dear?"

The tone was a caress, and she melted towards it, smiling up at him pitifully. "Phoebe to marry, and Tom no doubt spending much of his time in London! They no longer need me, Harry — I am cast aside and quite, quite useless."

He took both her hands in a firm grasp and looked earnestly into her eyes. "They've quitted the nest, Ianthe, as is the way of nature, but you have still a life of your own to lead. There is one here who needs you — has always needed you. Will you permit me to speak?"

She had cast down her eyes, as bashful as any maiden, but she still allowed him to retain her hands.

Encouraged by this, he continued. "I think you know that I've loved you since first we met, Ianthe. The years have brought no change in me, though my best friend Chalgrove was fortunate enough to win you. Since his death I've often wished to declare myself, but feared to lose the friendship which had grown between us. But now, when you feel the ties of your old life slackening, I am emboldened to hope that you might consider a new life with me, installed as mistress of the house which you're helping to turn into a home. Could you —" his voice trembled a little, strong man though he was — "could you find a little affection for me in your heart, my love, sufficient for you to take me as your husband?"

She made no answer for a moment, and his hopes faded.

"If you need time to consider —" he said, a muscle twitching in his cheek.

Ianthe Chalgrove was enjoying herself. She had known, of course, that he loved her, and that she could lay claim to him at any moment she chose, but there was a particular gratification in being addressed by an ardent — and still very personable — suitor, just as if one were a young girl again. It quite routed all her former feelings of rejection on her family's account.

And then, as she raised her eyes to his, a warmer emotion filled her. She was so very fond of dear Harry, the loyal friend who had been her comfort and stay ever since her husband's death. She knew she could be happy as his wife, and told him so, very prettily.

CHAPTER XIII

Three days after her impulsive return to Sussex, Eleanor was out walking, revelling in the quiet beauty of fresh, green, daisy-starred meadows lit by bright sunshine. In such perfect weather she felt in no hurry to return to London. Balls and parties were splendid fun, of course, but the country suited her present mood.

In truth, she had been experiencing unaccustomed fits of abstraction during these last few days, moods in which she found herself dwelling on thoughts which she would have preferred to dismiss summarily as being too disturbing and confused for comfort. One such mood was upon her now, and even the calm smiling face of her own well-loved countryside could not dispel it.

Her reverie was interrupted by the sound of a vehicle approaching, so she moved closer in to the hedge. A moment later, a curricle swept into view, drawn by a familiar pair of bay horses. She looked up at the driver and recognised Frederick Eversley.

He reined in his pair and touched his hat to her. "Morning, Miss Denham. Dashed near ran you down this time, for a change. I was coming to see you, though."

"To see me?" she repeated. "I must say, it's a surprise to see you here, sir. I had thought you to be in town. By the way, I must thank you for delivering my note to my sister. I heard from her this morning."

"Don't mention it — always happy to oblige," he replied, with a pleasant smile. "Are you going anywhere in particular, ma'am? May I offer you a lift?"

"I was just out for a stroll." She hesitated a moment, then asked, "Why did you wish to see me?"

"Oh, to hear how my cousins fared, ma'am, and if Tom brought the business off all right. At least, that was one reason," he added evasively.

"But have you not been to Chalgrove Park?" she asked, in surprise.

He shook his head, laughing. "Thought I'd see you first and find out how the land lies. But we can't talk like this — won't you step up into the curricle, ma'am?" He bent down and extended a hand. After a second's hesitation, she took it and climbed up beside him. "There, that's better," he said, with a satisfied air. "Shall I drive you home?"

She assented, and he gave his horses the office to start.

"Now, tell me what happened," he demanded. "I'm all agog."

"You'll be amazed, I think, when you know," she said, laughing. "Phoebe saw me yesterday and told me the whole story. To cut a long story short, Tom was all set to do battle with his mother, but the wind was quite taken out of his sails, for she agreed to everything. You'll never guess why!"

"Then I shan't waste time in attempting it," he returned, eyeing her quizzically. "Come, ma'am, pray don't keep me in suspense!"

"Lady Chalgrove," she said dramatically, "has become betrothed to Lord Ashcroft only a few days since."

Freddy emitted a whistle. "That certainly is surprising news."

"Of course, everybody knows he has been in love with her for ages," went on Eleanor. "It seems she has been assisting him in refurbishing Staplewood Court while your cousins have been away, and I suppose one thing led to another."

"He seems to have played his cards well — though, mind you, I don't envy anyone who takes on my Aunt Ianthe! Still, no accounting for tastes in such matters. So that leaves Tom undisputed master of Chalgrove Park. What of Phoebe?"

"Oh, she's in raptures, for she has permission to become betrothed to Geoffrey Lydhurst at last. It seems her mama feared that she might accept Viscount St. Keyne and go off to live in Northumberland — which Lady Chalgrove appears to consider as remote as the North Pole — so anything was considered preferable to that. But it was just a rumour, for Phoebe has never swerved from her attachment to Geoffrey, as I well know. Of course, Lady Chalgrove would infinitely have preferred you for Phoebe," she concluded, with a saucy look.

"Flattering though her preference may be," he said, with a grimace, "I can't think how she came by it, for I've a notion my aunt never liked me much."

"Oh, but it wasn't for that reason," explained Eleanor. "She wished for a family connection so that she might keep Phoebe close to her, you know."

Freddy shuddered. "I can only be thankful to have escaped such a fate. Not that there was the remotest possibility of its coming to pass — my cousin and I never had the faintest interest in each other. She's a sweet girl, of course, but not quite in my style."

"And then you have frequently said that you're a confirmed bachelor, in any event," Eleanor reminded him, with a sidelong glance.

He darted a quick look at her, but she was staring demurely ahead once more as they turned into the gates of Eastridge House. "Yes, well, I've come to think differently of late," he replied, giving undue attention to taking his curricle along the short drive.

"Indeed?" murmured Eleanor politely. Then, as they drew nearer the house, she added, "You may as well take the curricle round to the stables, for you'll come indoors, will you not?"

"Yes, thank you — that is, if I won't be intruding?" His tone was unusually diffident, and she gave a secret smile, feeling a small sense of power that was not unpleasing. She had a score to settle with Mr. Eversley, and this seemed to be a propitious moment for it.

"I suppose it would be premature to wish you happy?" she asked wickedly.

"Unfortunately, yes." The reply was terse.

"But one can't help wondering, you know," she continued in the same tone, "just what kind of female is in your style."

He turned such an intense look upon her that all the mischief died out of her face and she felt her heart hammering. "One very like you," he said, in a low voice.

She had known for some days in her heart of hearts that he was the man for her, though until now she had refused to acknowledge it. She had suspected that her feelings were reciprocated, while dreading that she might be mistaken. Even so, she was not prepared to capitulate immediately. She dared to gamble with her hopes by making him wait for his answer. "You mean one who deliberately schemes to make a brilliant match?" she asked provocatively.

The curricle had by now arrived in the stableyard, and several grooms came forward to take charge of it. There could not have been a more awkward moment for continuing the conversation, so he made no attempt to reply.

Before Freddy could jump down and assist Eleanor to alight, one of the grooms had already performed this office. Directions were given as to the disposal of the vehicle, then the two turned away to walk towards the house.

For several moments silence fell between them, then he glanced at her somewhat apprehensively.

"I knew you'd want to tackle me over that," he said at last, in a resigned tone.

"Well, you might," she replied tartly. "With such an opinion of my character, I wonder you wish to continue your acquaintance with me at all."

"But I haven't — I mean, I hadn't," he protested. "No, dash it all, that's not what I mean at all!" He paused in order to sort out his thoughts so that he might present his case more creditably, but she gave him no chance for this.

"'Tis of small interest to me what you do or do not mean," she said loftily. "Your opinion of me is of no account."

He stole a look at her half-averted face and found no encouragement there. He sighed. "A pity, for I'd have liked to explain — still, since you feel as you do, no doubt you're anxious to be rid of me. No point now in my accompanying you into the house. I'll bid you goodbye, Miss Denham." He bowed and was about to turn away, but she raised a hand to stop him.

"One moment, sir. I, at any rate, will not be guilty of condemning anyone too hastily. Little difference though I think it can make, I will at least hear your explanation."

He looked down into her face with a steady, serious gaze which set her pulses fluttering once more. "I'll give it to you in one word," he said quietly. "Jealousy. I didn't realise it then, when I was insulting you with those insinuations about being on the catch for an earl, but I had good cause later to understand my motives. Everything I had known of you up to that time had shown me that you were warm-hearted and impulsive, not cold and calculating — that such despicable tricks were beneath you! Yet something forced me on to accuse you falsely in spite of myself. It didn't take me very long to find the answer."

They had both stopped on the path and now stood facing each other, Eleanor with her head bent because she could not for the moment meet his eyes.

"I suppose it's no use?" he asked dubiously. "You couldn't possibly return my regard?"

She looked up at him then; a mischievous smile played about her lips, but her eyes were tender. "I might," she whispered, "if you were to try very hard to persuade me."

He caught her in his arms. "Oh, Nell, dearest, I love you to distraction!"

Her foot slipped on the gravel, and he held her yet tighter.

The sound of footsteps behind them made them start guiltily apart. Sir George stood quizzically regarding them.

"How do you do, sir?" said Freddy, tugging at his cravat. "I wanted to see you — to ask permission to pay my addresses to your daughter."

"Hm!" Sir George grinned. "Seems to me you're doing well enough without it."

"My foot slipped on the gravel, Papa," explained Eleanor shyly. "That was why —"

"Oh, aye, puss, I dare say!" he replied, chucking her under the chin. "What do you say to this young fellow? Do you wish to wed him, eh?"

"Yes, if you please, Papa," said Nell demurely.

"Well, that's all right then," her father announced, with a laugh. "Come along indoors, and we'll break the good news to your mother. Tell you what, Eversley," he added, as he tucked Nell's arm in his, "when a man's been blessed with six daughters, he's glad to welcome any eligible gentleman who's willing to take another of them off his hands, what?"

A NOTE TO THE READER

If you have enjoyed the novel enough to leave a review on **Amazon** and **Goodreads**, then we would be truly grateful.

Sapere Books is an exciting new publisher of brilliant fiction and popular history.

To find out more about our latest releases and our monthly bargain books visit our website: **saperebooks.com**

Printed in Great Britain
by Amazon

82568672R00092